K19 SECURITY SOLUTIONS
TEAM TWO
—BOOK THREE—

USA TODAY BESTSELLING AUTHOR
HEATHER SLADE

MORE FROM AUTHOR HEATHER SLADE

BUTLER RANCH
Kade's Worth
Brodie's Promise
Maddox's Truce
Naughton's Secret
Mercer's Vow
Kade's Return
Butler Ranch Christmas

WICKED WINEMAKERS
FIRST LABEL
Brix's Bid
Ridge's Release
Press' Passion
Zin's Sins
Tryst's Temptation

WICKED WINEMAKERS
SECOND LABEL
Beau's Beloved
Coming Soon:
Cru's Crush
Bones' Bliss
Snapper's Seduction
Kick's Kiss

ROARING FORK RANCH
Coming Soon:
Roaring Fork Wrangler
Roaring Fork Roughstock
Roaring Fork Rockstar
Roaring Fork Rooker
Roaring Fork Bridger

THE ROYAL AGENTS
OF MI6
Make Me Shiver
Drive Me Wilder
Feel My Pinch
Chase My Shadow
Find My Angel

K19 SECURITY
SOLUTIONS TEAM ONE
Razor's Edge
Gunner's Redemption
Mistletoe's Magic
Mantis' Desire
Dutch's Salvation

K19 SECURITY
SOLUTIONS TEAM TWO
Striker's Choice
Monk's Fire
Halo's Oath
Tackle's Honor
Onyx's Awakening

K19 SHADOW OPERATIONS
TEAM ONE
Code Name: Ranger
Code Name: Diesel
Code Name: Wasp
Code Name: Cowboy
Code Name: Mayhem

K19 ALLIED INTELLIGENCE
TEAM ONE
Code Name: Ares
Code Name: Cayman
Code Name: Poseidon
Code Name: Zeppelin
Code Name: Magnet

K19 ALLIED INTELLIGENCE
TEAM TWO
Coming Soon:
Code Name: Puck
Code Name: Michelangelo
Code Name: Typhon
Code Name: Hornet
Code Name: Reaper

PROTECTORS
UNDERCOVER
Undercover Agent
Undercover Emissary
Coming Soon:
Undercover Savior
Undercover Infidel
Undercover Assassin

THE INVINCIBLES
TEAM ONE
Decked
Edged
Grinded
Riled
Smoked

THE INVINCIBLES
TEAM TWO
Bucked
Irished
Sainted
Hammered
Ripped

THE UNSTOPPABLES
TEAM ONE
Furied
Merried

COWBOYS OF
CRESTED BUTTE
A Cowboy Falls
A Cowboy's Dance
A Cowboy's Kiss
A Cowboy Stays
A Cowboy Wins

Table of Contents

1

Halo

I'd been on this assignment since March. Eight months of this shit. Stuck in some small-ass town on the Oregon Coast, surveilling a woman who made watching grass grow seem interesting.

In contrast, last Thanksgiving, I wasn't sure I'd make it out of Somalia alive. My partner, Tackle, and I were undercover as journalists when we were kidnapped by a band of pirates.

It didn't take the team the CIA sent in long to rescue us, but I didn't make it home in time to celebrate Thanksgiving with my family. When I hit US soil a couple of days after, though, I seriously thought about kneeling down and kissing the ground.

Those were the extremes of the line of work I was in. Either I was in danger of losing my life, or I was bored out of my mind.

"You can head home," Griffin "Striker" Ellis said when I called him to give him an update on the woman he was paying me to keep an eye on—Aine McNamara.

Striker had been the lead on the team that rescued Tackle and me, and while none of us worked for the CIA anymore, it didn't change the fact I owed the man my life. When he asked me to keep tabs on the woman he'd recently ended a relationship with, I didn't hesitate to say yes.

Said woman had been kidnapped in August of last year, a couple of months before I was in Somalia. I knew Striker still felt responsible for making sure she was safe. I didn't understand why they'd broken up in the first place, since they both seemed like they still cared for each other. That part wasn't any of my business, though.

"I'm sure you want to spend Thanksgiving with your family."

Did I? Barring any other option, I supposed so.

"By the way, I heard that K19 is getting ready to make you an offer."

Bingo! I'd been hoping they would since the day I left the CIA. I'd almost given up, deciding that if I didn't hear from them by January, I'd start looking at other firms that handled covert operations.

Striker wasn't just the lead on my rescue; he'd also been my boss back when we were both with the agency. When he left their employ, I did too. In hindsight, my departure may have been premature, but you had to know who had your back in this line of work and who didn't.

Outside of Striker, there were only a handful of men and women I trusted, and not a single one still worked for the government in an official capacity. In fact, the majority of them were now part of a black ops and intelligence firm called K19 Security Solutions, the one Striker had just said was getting ready to make me an offer.

"What about Tackle?" I asked.

"Him too."

Landry "Tackle" Sorenson was more than my partner on the op in Somalia; he and I had been best friends since high school when my family returned to America after living in England for most of my childhood.

Tackle and I attended the same college, University of Virginia, and went on to accept jobs with the CIA after we graduated. While it was common for a place like the Central Intelligence Agency to assign code names, my friend and I already had them—nicknames anyway—that to our surprise, they'd agreed to allow us to use.

We'd come up with them after a day of playing touch football when things went a little too far. It wouldn't be difficult for anyone to figure out that Landry had tackled me or that I ended up with a cervical dislocation requiring I wear a neck halo for six weeks.

While Landry and his parents felt like absolute shit about it, I wasn't angry nor were my mom and dad. Accidents happened, they'd said. I think they were just relieved that the injury hadn't been worse. It didn't bother them at all I couldn't play football the next year, and while I acted like I was disappointed, I'd admitted to Tackle that I didn't really care.

The day I told him I planned to resign from the CIA and freelance for K19, he said he would too.

"Where are you?" I asked when my friend answered my call.

"On my way to Boston."

Tackle and I lived in DC, but both sets of our parents lived in Newton, Massachusetts.

"I was thinking of doing the same."

"Striker isn't making you babysit over the holiday?"

I told him about the call I'd just hung up from and also about the impending offer.

"About damn time," he muttered. "When do you get in?"

"I haven't booked the flight yet, but I'll let you know as soon as I do."

"Roger that. I land at four this afternoon."

"I'll see what I can arrange."

Tackle offered to pick me up whenever I landed, which I was sure my parents would appreciate. More, my younger sister would, since she was the one who usually got stuck doing airport runs.

"It was nice of you to bring Knox home," my mother said to Tackle the next day when he dropped me off at my parents' place and came inside.

She put her arms around me. "I can't believe you'll actually be with us for the holiday this year."

My father, Benjamin Knox Clarkson, Sr., an American, had never cared much about holidays. He'd worked for the State Department most of his life, traveling the world. However, my mother, who was Venezuelan, loved holidays—any holiday. Almost too much, overly embracing decorating for any occasion. Presently, my parents' house looked like it had been the venue for a pilgrim party.

"There are six days between now and then," I said. "Don't tempt fate."

I don't know who should've kept their mouth shut—her or me—but here it was, the day before Thanksgiving, and both Tackle and I were on a transport to Atlanta. There, we'd be on standby until we were given the word to connect with Montano "Onyx" Yáñez and fly to Bogotá.

Once we arrived in Columbia's capital, I'd be going undercover into one of the drug cartels while Tackle was positioned inside the US embassy.

Hadn't I just been wishing for a mission more interesting than watching over Aine McNamara? I scrubbed my face. *Be careful what you wish for.*

The next afternoon, we received our orders and boarded a plane belonging to K19. Onyx was piloting, and another operative I'd heard of but never worked with, Sofia "Corazón" Descanso, was his copilot.

We'd been in the air for almost five hours and were just past Aruba when all hell broke loose.

Tackle and I jumped up from our seats and raced to the cockpit when we heard a shot being fired. When we slammed through the door, guns cocked, Onyx was slumped over the plane's instrument panel and Corazón had her gun pointed directly at me.

Either way, I was going to die today—if I fired first, the unmanned plane would crash. If I let her shoot me, she'd kill Tackle too, and then she may have a chance of getting away with a triple murder. I pulled the trigger.

2

Tara

Why in the hell did I come to California for Thanksgiving? I'd only done it so I didn't have to be alone. But here I was, surrounded by people, four of my best friends in the world, and I'd never felt more alone in my life.

From the time we were seven years old—when we all showed up at the same boarding school—until just recently, we'd been the Tribe of Five, always looking out for each other in a way no one else did. All of our parents—to one degree or another—had lives that didn't include much time for child-rearing. That's why we'd banded together in the first place. Shared misery, loneliness, and a profound sense of abandonment.

I couldn't pinpoint exactly when Quinn, Ava, Aine, Penelope, and I had started to grow apart. More and more, I felt like I no longer connected with the four of them. I couldn't say or do the right thing—ever. What we all used to find funny became me being a bitch…or immature.

Part of it was that, in the last year, our lives had all gone in different directions. Quinn got married first; Ava followed not long after her. Penelope got a job she loved, as a physical therapist, and Aine had been in a committed relationship that, while she said they'd broken up, seemed as though it was back on.

That left me. I had a degree in art history and no idea what to do with it. Sure, I could work in a museum, but where I'd have to start would bore me to tears. It wasn't like I could show up and immediately get a job as a curator. I'd have to start as a curatorial assistant. No, thanks.

I noticed the key fob for the rental car sitting on the counter, picked it up, and sneaked it into my pocket, wondering if I left, how long it would be before anyone even noticed I was gone. Or maybe they would notice and be thankful.

Even I had to admit I was bitchy. Ever since Pen and I decided at the last minute to fly here for the holiday and a couple of my credit cards were declined, I'd been distracted. I called my dad before we left to find out why, but so far, he hadn't returned my call.

Pen had offered to cover the cost of the airfare, just so we could get the flights booked and be on our way, which wasn't that big of a deal. I just hated having something like this hanging over my head.

When my phone vibrated with a call from a friend I'd known even longer than the four I was here with, I crept out the front door. "Hey, Brand," I said. "Can I call you right back?"

"Of course. Where are you?"

"California. I'll explain in a few minutes."

I drove the rental car over to the beach, parked, and returned the call.

"What are you doing in California?"

"Celebrating the holiday with the tribe."

"Right. It's Thanksgiving, isn't it?"

"What's up?"

"There's something I need to talk to you about."

"Aren't we talking now?"

"Not over the phone."

"What's going on?"

"Let me know when you're back in New York. We'll talk then."

When the call ended, I walked down to the beach. There weren't many people out today, but no one other than me was alone. I sat down, lay back in the sand, and closed my eyes, wishing I could shake the feeling that something was wrong. Something far worse than my declined credit card.

I must've dozed off. When I checked the time, I was shocked at how late it had gotten. I traipsed up the steps to where I'd parked the car and drove back to the house.

"Where in the hell have you been?" Pen shouted when I walked in the front door.

"What the fuck?" I shouted back. She was my roommate, not my goddamn mother.

"You left without a word to anyone. You wouldn't answer your phone. We were worried about you."

I laughed. "Right. How long did it take before you even noticed I wasn't here?"

"Look," said Pen, lowering her voice. "We know about your father."

I stopped dead in my tracks. "What about him?"

"Don't play stupid. The investigation."

"I don't know what you're talking about."

"Come sit," said Aine, motioning to me.

"I have to call my dad." I rushed out to the deck and closed the sliding door behind me.

Of course, it went to voicemail, so I called my mom.

"Where are you?" she asked.

"California."

After the requisite niceties, I asked if she'd heard anything from my dad.

"Your father stopped being my responsibility a long time ago, Tara." Why had I called her? Really, what had I expected?

"I heard something about an investigation."

"You *heard* something? Tara, it's all over the news. You want answers, ask him."

"I've been trying to reach him. He isn't returning my calls."

"Ask Vi. She knows more about your father than any-one. That was true even when he and I were married."

Vi! Why hadn't I thought of that? I ended the call with my mother after wishing her a happy holiday and called Viola Ripa, the woman who had been my father's secretary since before I was born.

I wasn't surprised when that call went to voicemail too. It was a national holiday, after all.

I sat down at the table and searched for my father's name on the internet. While my mother had said it was "all over the news," I couldn't find anything other than a mention in the *Times* that one of his companies was under investigation for wire fraud. Was that really a big deal? I supposed, coupled with my credit cards being declined, I should be more concerned.

I tried my father one more time, but like a few minutes earlier, the call went straight to voicemail.

I hated asking Pen for help again, but it looked like the best thing for me to do was get back to New York. I quickly changed my mind when I opened the door in time to hear her say, "It's almost like she's on something."

On something? I eased it the rest of the way and went inside.

"What is that supposed to mean? I'm 'on something' because I decided I needed some time on my own? By the way, thanks for blindsiding me. I hope you're all happy now."

"Wait a minute," said Pen, standing. "No one blindsided you, and why would any of us be happy your father is being investigated?"

"I need to get back to New York."

"So go." Pen sat back down.

"Come with me." Quinn took my hand and pulled me out the front door. "What's up?"

"Didn't you hear? I'm *on* something."

"Don't be like that. I'm trying to help you. What's happening with your dad?"

I told her about my conversation with my mother and what I'd found on the internet, not that it was much.

"What do you want to do?" she asked.

"I've been trying to reach my dad since yesterday. I really feel like I should go home."

"Are you sure? I mean, what can you do there that you couldn't do here?"

For starters, not be judged by people who I thought loved me?

"I have to see him."

"Okay. If you're absolutely certain." Quinn put her hand on my arm. "I know Pen paid for your ticket here. I'll take care of you getting back to New York. And you're not asking; I'm offering." Quinn opened the door, and I followed her back inside. "I'm giving Tara a ride to the airport," she said to Aine and Pen. I didn't see Ava.

"Bye," I said, waving behind me, wishing I hadn't even come back in.

"Wait," Pen called out. "How about a hug? And what about Aine?"

"And what about Ava?" Aine asked after I hugged her and Pen.

"Tell her I said thank you."

We arrived at the small airport in San Luis Obispo a few minutes before the last flight out for the day. It was going to LAX, but from there, I could catch a flight to JFK.

"Bye, and thank you," I said, hugging Quinn.

"Here," she said, shoving something in my purse.

"What is that?"

"Cash."

"I can't." I reached in to give it back to her.

"Just take it." She kissed my cheek. "Go, or you'll miss your flight."

When I landed at JFK at six in the morning, there was a voicemail from a number I didn't recognize. "Tara, it's Vi Ripa. I got your message. It's urgent I see you as soon as possible. Meet me at your father's apartment as soon as you get this."

It was just after eight when I walked into the lobby of my dad's building. Twelve hours later, I was on a plane heading to Europe, traveling under an assumed identity, with twenty grand in cash and a burner phone.

3

Halo

When I opened my eyes, I was in a hospital. How in the hell was I even alive? The plane had crashed.

"Where am I?" I asked when a woman walked into the room.

"Foundation University Hospital Metropolitano," she answered with a strong South American accent. "You are a very lucky man to survive with so few injuries."

"Were there…others?"

"One is in the room next door; one is in the ICU."

"They lived? We all lived?" I mumbled. "I am alive, right?"

She set the clipboard she was holding down on the table by the side of the bed and smiled. "Yes, you are alive, but I'm going to check your vitals just to be sure."

"How long have I been here?"

"Just a few hours. While you have several broken bones and suffered a head injury, you did not require surgery."

"Are you certain?"

She took the stethoscope out of her ears. "About which part?"

"That I didn't need surgery?" It sure as hell felt like I should have.

Before she could answer, the door burst open and Razor Sharp, one of K19 Security Solutions' founding partners, rushed in.

"How is he?" he asked the nurse.

"Alive, which seems to surprise him."

"Nothing wrong with my hearing."

Razor came over to the bed and rested his hand on my arm. "Thank God you're going to be okay."

"She said one of the other victims is next door and another in the ICU. Do you know their condition?" I asked once the woman left the room.

"Tackle is about as banged up as you are. Onyx, though, he's in bad shape."

"Corazón shot him."

"We've been able to piece that together." Razor pulled up a chair and sat. "We have plenty of time for a hotwash later."

"What happens now?"

"We wait for Onyx's condition to stabilize enough that he can be transported back to the States."

"Can I see him?"

Razor shook his head. "Not yet, but I heard a rumor that Tackle may be able to mobilize sooner than you."

A few days later, we were released to return to America. Onyx was being transported to George Washington University Hospital in DC. I'd need to see a doctor stateside for a follow-up, so would Tackle, but as it stood now, neither of us would need to be admitted unless we developed complications.

"I'm going to tell as many people as I can that I love them," I said to Tackle, who was in the seat next to me on the flight home.

He nodded. "Me too."

"Even my extended family. My aunts and uncles will all think I'm nuts, but I don't give a shit."

"Huge wake-up call," Tackle muttered.

"Can I ask you something?"

"Shoot."

"You ever think about settling down, getting married, having kids?"

"I didn't before."

"It's different now, right?"

He nodded. "Is there anyone you've been, you know, seeing?"

His question stunned me. If I had been, he sure as hell would've known about it. "Negative. What about you?"

"There's someone."

"There is?" And I didn't know about her? I was even more stunned. "Who is she?"

"That isn't important right now. If or when that changes, I'll let you know."

What the fuck? "Seriously?"

"She might not feel the same way I do."

"Is it someone I know?"

Tackle shook his head, but he was lying. Who could it be that he didn't want to tell me? There was no one I could think of.

I rested my head against the back of the seat. What about me? I hadn't been on many dates since the kidnapping in Somalia. The few I had, left me feeling less connected rather than more. Consequently, there hadn't been many second dates, and fewer, if any, thirds.

I was thirty-two years old, with a career that kept me traveling the globe, living in a place where people who worked for the agency made up the bulk of the population. How in the hell would I ever meet someone I could spend enough time with to even get to know, let alone share a life with?

Like I said to Tackle, I felt different now, coming as close to death as we had. I wanted my life to have purpose, meaning, not just in my job, but outside of it too.

If I thought about the men and women I worked with at K19, most of them were involved with other agents or, in Razor's case, someone whose detail he covered. Since the only detail I'd done recently was for my boss' ex-girlfriend, that wasn't exactly a hotbed of possibilities either. Online dating? With what I did? No way. Not even an option.

The question I'd asked Tackle—whether he'd ever thought about settling down, getting married, having kids—was something I'd been thinking about since the morning I woke up, stunned that I was still alive.

I'd talked to my parents and sister, but once those conversations ended and I realized there was no one else for me to call, it left me feeling like there was something big missing in my life.

When we landed at the airfield in DC, my parents and sister were there, waiting with Tackle's family.

My mother embraced me a little too hard, and I flinched but didn't say anything. I could only imagine how she'd felt when she heard I was in a plane crash.

My dad rarely showed much emotion, but today he did, as did my sister. Once they'd all hugged me, we switched, and they hugged Tackle in the same way his family loved on me.

We'd spent so much time at each other's houses when we were growing up that our parents ended up being good friends too.

I turned around when Tackle's mother released me, and caught the tail end of him embracing my sister. There was something weird about it, especially when Sloane looked right at me as though she wondered if I'd seen them. Tackle's words echoed in my head. "She might not feel the same way I do." It couldn't be, though, could it? Nah, Sloane was as much his little sister as she was mine. Except for biology. I continued to watch them both, but they appeared to be ignoring each other now.

"I want you to come home for a while," said my mother when we walked into the terminal building. I couldn't fathom sitting through another flight, not to mention I wanted to stay here in Washington so I could monitor Onyx's condition.

I was surprised when, later, I overheard Tackle say he was planning to go to Boston.

"Just for a few days," he said when I asked him about it.

It wasn't up to me to tell him he should stay here. That was his decision to make, just like it was mine.

Most days, for the next month, I went to the hospital to see Onyx. Not as often as Rhys "Monk" Perrin did, though. He was there almost around the clock, waiting for Onyx to come out of the coma he'd been in since we were rescued in Columbia.

Monk had been the handler on the mission, and no matter who or how many times the K19 team tried to convince him the plane crash was in no way his fault, he still felt responsible.

It wasn't until right before Christmas that Monk asked about it. Tackle and I were both headed to Boston to spend the holidays with our families, but stopped by the hospital first. We'd been there an hour and were getting ready to leave when he offered to walk us out.

"I'm sure you've already briefed Doc about this, but what went down that day?" he asked.

Tackle rubbed the back of his neck with his hand. "It was a major Charlie Foxtrot, Monk."

I nodded. "I don't know what went on in the cockpit, but when we were just past Aruba, all hell broke loose." I closed my eyes, reliving the day I was sure I was going to die. "It all happened so fast. We heard a shot being fired and stormed the front of the plane. Onyx had taken a direct hit, and Corazón had her gun turned our way when I fired."

"By that time, the plane was already taking a dive. I didn't think there was any way we'd live through it," Tackled added.

"I'll tell you what. Every day since we've been home, I've told as many people as I can that I love them. The other thing is, life is too fucking short to not have someone you love by your side. I know that isn't easy to find, but when I do, I'm gonna make damn sure I don't waste any time."

Tackle nodded. "I feel the same way. Any time I find myself thinking I'll put something off until the next day, I stop and do whatever it is right then. I came too damn close to not having any more next days."

He didn't mention the woman he'd talked about on our way back from Columbia, making me suspect it hadn't worked out after all.

We'd just stepped off the elevator in the parking garage when a call came in from Striker. I knew why he was calling, and it wasn't something I'd discussed with Tackle.

"You got a minute?" he asked.

"Tackle and I are about to head to the airfield."

"I'll meet you there."

"What was that about?" Tackle asked.

"I've decided not to accept K19's offer."

He'd started the car but cut the engine. "Why not?"

"You can drive." I motioned for him to restart the car.

Tackle shook his head. "Why not?" he repeated.

"I gave it a lot of thought, and I'm just not ready to make that kind of commitment."

"What are you going to do?"

"I don't know yet, but maybe some PI work."

My friend nodded, turning his head so I couldn't see his face. "Tell him you need more time."

"What about you? Have you given them an answer?"

"No."

Neither Doc Butler nor his wife, Merrigan, the managing partners of K19 Security Solutions, had pressured me about the junior partnership offer they'd extended shortly before the mission that took us to Columbia. Striker was the only person from the firm who'd asked if I'd made a decision. I assumed the same was true for Tackle.

"What about you? What are you going to do?"

"I'm thinking about working for my dad."

Tackle's father owned a construction company where we'd both worked during high school summer vacations.

"Is that what you did, told them you needed more time?"

He nodded.

"Nothing like surviving a plane crash to make a guy reassess his life."

Tackle laughed. "Listen, I'm sorry I've been so distant."

"We okay?"

"Always."

He said the word, but I wasn't feeling it. I didn't call him out on it, though. I was going through enough shit of my own to get that he was too.

When we got to the airfield, Striker was waiting.

"I'll be in the bar," said Tackle after greeting the man who had been our boss at the CIA and, to a certain extent, still was.

"I want you to take some more time before you give K19 a hard pass."

"Tackle gave me the same advice."

"No one expects a decision right away, Halo. Not after what you've been through."

"I appreciate that."

"There is a job I want to talk to you about, though."

I shifted on my feet, really wishing he wasn't about to offer me something I wasn't ready to take on.

"It's a missing-person case."

"Who's missing?"

"Tara Emsworth."

"Name sounds familiar."

"She's a good friend of Aine's. One of her best, actually. She disappeared the same day as the plane crash."

"Don't like that reminder."

"Why I told you right off."

Tackle said the same thing about Tara's name sounding familiar when I met him in the bar and told him about the job Striker had offered me.

"She's one of Razor's wife's best friends."

"Right. Mercer's wife's too." Both men were K19 founding partners.

While on the flight home, Tackle helped me craft a plan of action to find Emsworth and offered to help.

"You wanna come in?" I asked when he pulled up to my parents' house in the car he'd left at Logan when he last flew to DC.

"I'll be over later."

"Right." I got out of the car, hoping that after a few days here, our friendship would get back on track.

4

Tara

It had been almost three years since I was in Europe, and there were so many places I wished I could visit—cities I'd been to before when the tribe and I backpacked all over the continent during college. *We* were five then. Now, *they* were four, since I had no idea when I might be returning to the States and, even when I did, whether I'd get in touch with them.

I was still pissed at Penelope for saying she thought I was "on something." What I was "on" was the same thing I knew she was—anti-anxiety medication. I hadn't asked, but I wouldn't be surprised if Ava and Aine were on it too.

After what had happened to us last year, how could they not be? Who could survive being kidnapped and then not fear it might happen again?

It was shortly after Quinn's wedding that Aine, Penelope, and I had been taken hostage by a group of Armenians. Who they'd really wanted was Ava, but got her twin, Aine, instead. Since Pen and I were with her, we were collateral damage.

The kidnappers kept us drugged and moved us from San Francisco to Seattle. We were rescued after three days, but the nightmares still remained. I'd never been so terrified in my life. The medication I took helped a little, as did therapy. Not that I'd be able to continue with either now that I was operating under an assumed identity.

I was sure my therapist would be worried when I didn't show up for my appointment next week, and maybe Pen would be as well when she got home from the West Coast and discovered I took most of my things out of the apartment we shared.

After the plane landed and I'd gotten through customs without incident, I went to the train station and bought a ticket to Heidelberg.

My plan was to head to Stuttgart after a few days and then go into Switzerland through Zürich. There, I would withdraw money from the bank account set up in the name of Catarina Benedetto—my alias.

***

I'd been in Europe almost four weeks, and tomorrow was Christmas. I'd be spending it in a *pensione* in Bellano, a small town on the eastern shore of Lake Como.

I'd been invited to join my hosts and fellow travelers for a holiday meal, but I'd declined. I was in no mood for socializing or trying to pretend I wasn't heartbroken to be spending Christmas alone.

5

Halo

I didn't start my search for Tara Emsworth in earnest until after New Year's Day.

She'd been missing since Thanksgiving when she got on a plane to fly from Los Angeles to JFK. The manifest said she was on the flight, but no one had seen or heard from her after it landed. At least no one willing to come forward.

She was the victim of a messy divorce between a mother and father who, it appeared, didn't pay a whole lot of attention to her other than to give her money. Attempts to reach her father had gone unanswered. When I contacted her mother, the only thing she could tell me was that Tara had always been daddy's little girl and she had no idea where her daughter was. Probably gallivanting around the globe with her ex-husband.

Classic poor little rich girl except, now, she was missing, and God knew how long she'd been gone.

In the last week, I'd checked jails, hospitals, and morgues, along with interviewing her friends and reviewing social media accounts.

I was sitting in a coffee shop across from the building where Tara's father kept an apartment when my cell rang with a call from one of my contacts still at the CIA, Money McTiernan. I'd contacted him a few days ago to see if he could help me get access to Tara's financial records.

"Some information hit my desk this morning that might prove useful in your search for Tara Emsworth."

"Go ahead."

"It's about her father. Richard Emsworth was about to be indicted when he disappeared."

"For?"

"Wire fraud, mainly, but to the tune of millions of dollars. The thing that makes it even more interesting is there is also a pending enterprise corruption charge."

Enterprise corruption was defined as participating in a pattern of criminal activity and knowingly investing proceeds from that conduct into another enterprise. The charge was typically a euphemism for the accused having ties to organized crime, specifically, the Mafia.

"You said he disappeared. When was that?" I asked.

"The last confirmed report of his whereabouts was from the day before Thanksgiving."

"Tara went missing that day."

"You think they took off together?"

"That's one theory. Why'd it hit your desk?"

"In addition to the investigation here in the States, AISE has their own inquisition into Emsworth's crimes. My guess is I'll be hearing from Interpol next."

The *Agenzia Informazioni e Sicurezza Esterna*, or AISE as Money referred to them, was Italy's version of the CIA. Interpol, whose official abbreviation was ICPO-INTERPOL, was the international organization that facilitated worldwide police cooperation and crime control.

"Is CIA involvement official, then?"

"Just waiting for final sign-off."

"Thanks, Money."

"Halo, there's one more thing. It's actually the reason for my call. You asked about the daughter's financial records."

"Did you find anything?"

"At the same time the indictment was about to be handed down, the father's assets were frozen. I started tracking his prior money trail, and while he's covered his tracks pretty damn well, something turned up in Switzerland. Right before Christmas, a young woman matching Tara's description came in and made a significant cash withdrawal."

When my call ended with McTiernan, I immediately called Striker and relayed what I'd learned.

"This presents an interesting scenario, doesn't it?" Striker murmured.

"How do you want me to proceed?"

"Let me get back to you on that."

I was still sitting in the same coffee shop, studying the photos that were part of the dossier I'd been given on Tara, when Striker called back.

"I had Doc contact McTiernan, and we've been approved to conduct a 'fact-finding mission' on Emsworth, officially the father, on behalf of the CIA."

I sent a silent plea, hoping he was about to tell me I'd been assigned to it. Sure enough, my prayer was answered.

"Where am I headed?"

"Italy. Tuscany, specifically."

6

Tara

I'd kept my old cell phone, even though I removed the SIM card, only for the messages on it that I'd saved as voice memos. One was from a woman I'd once considered my best friend.

On the days I felt homesick, I'd pull out the handful of things I'd kept to remind me of my once-charmed life, turn on the phone, and listen. It always did the trick. Not only couldn't I go back to the place I'd once considered home, but right now, I didn't want to.

Tonight was one of the times when I found myself hovering on the edge of missing maybe not my home, but the four friends who had been closer to me than anyone in my family.

The *pensione* in Sienna, where I was spending the night, was empty but for me, so I went ahead and got my phone out and hit play on the last message I got from Pen before disconnecting my cell service.

"Listen, Tara," it began. "As much as we love you, none of us appreciate that instead of asking for help we would have gladly given, you chose to steal from us. The money isn't important, but the bracelet you took from Aine is a family heirloom, and she's devastated to have lost something so precious. Maybe you could just make sure she gets that back."

I hadn't taken anything from them, except for the money Quinn put in my bag and insisted I keep. I certainly wouldn't have taken jewelry. That they'd so easily accused me, though, shattered my heart.

Any hope I'd held out that it was my imagination that we'd grown apart, dissipated in one voicemail. What stunned me almost more than anything else, was that Quinn had gone along with the accusations. She'd seen firsthand how upset and humiliated I was about my dad. How could she not have told Pen, Aine, and Ava that they had to be wrong?

Whether Aine found the bracelet, or they discovered someone else took it and the cash, or even if they'd called to apologize, I didn't know and might not for quite some time.

I cried myself to sleep like I seemed to be doing more and more lately. When I woke the next morning,

I decided to do something nice for myself and go wine tasting.

There hadn't been time for me to visit wineries the last time I was in Italy. Actually, there had been, but my four travel companions hadn't been interested, so I was outvoted. There were several I'd longed to see along the ancient consular route, Via Cassia, that passed through Val d'Orcia.

A tour company went to three that were in close proximity. Two, I'd never heard of, but the third was a place I'd always wanted to see—the *Antica Cascina dei Conti di Valentini*—which translated to the Ancient Farmhouse of the Counts of Valentini. From what I'd read, it was one of the few wineries remaining on the Via Cassia route that continued to produce wine the way it had been for hundreds of years. Many of the others had modernized, but they hadn't.

The group I went with was small, made up mainly of older Americans. Since I spoke fluent Italian, I simply apologized for my limited understanding of English and they left me alone.

I sighed and looked out the window of the bus. Just being in Val d'Orcia, in the Central Italian region of Tuscany, was enough to soothe my soul. The rich green valley, which encompassed the Orcia River, was the perfect place for me to escape my dark thoughts.

This area was said to be the jewel of Tuscany, with medieval castles, ancient villages, gorgeous farmhouses, isolated homesteads, roads lined with cypress trees, fabulous vineyards and olive groves, and golden fields of grain and sunflowers.

I'd traveled many places, all over the world, but none compared to this.

When we drove through the gates of Valentini, I put my hand on my heart. It was so beautiful, it nearly brought me to tears. It was everything I'd imagined it to be and so much more.

I lingered behind, letting the rest of the group make their way into the winery and get settled before I followed.

"*Buongiorno*, welcome to Valentini," said a woman, who looked to be about my age.

"It's so beautiful," I murmured, as much to myself as to her.

She came and stood beside me, taking in the same views I was. "It never fails to take my breath away, and I grew up here. I'm Pia Deltetto."

I studied her instead of the view. "It's so nice to meet you, Tara…err…Catarina Benedetto."

"Are you with the group?" She motioned to the tasting room.

I sighed. "Yes, I suppose I should go in." I realized she might think I wasn't interested in tasting their wine. "I mean, I've wanted to visit Valentini for years…just not necessarily with a group."

Pia smiled and looped her arm through mine. "For years? You look very young for your age, then. How about if we do a taste without the group?"

She led me into a small room off the main tasting area. "This is for our VIP customers," she said, winking. "At Valentini, we limit our production to—"

"Brunello di Montalcino and Rosso di Montalcino."

She raised a brow.

"I'm sorry I interrupted. Go ahead."

Pia poured two glasses from an unmarked Jeroboam.

"This is our latest vintage of Brunello di Montalcino," she said as we both swirled and sniffed.

I closed my eyes and sorted what I smelled in my head. Cherry and dried cranberry were predominant, with undertones of strawberry and blackberry. The fruit aromas blended with licorice and espresso. I took a sip, letting the wine linger on my palate.

While this wine was fantastic in its youth, aged Brunello, especially Valentini's, were my favorites. Give it a few years, and the flavors would intensify.

When I opened my eyes, Pia was studying me and smiling. "You like it?"

I shook my head. "I love it."

She squealed and clapped her hands. "You have a very discerning palate."

"I don't know about that, but I do know what I like."

"Me too," said Pia with a giggle when a tall, dark, and very handsome man walked into the main tasting room.

"Someone you know?" I asked.

"No. You?"

I shook my head. "I don't know anyone."

He looked in our direction briefly, and Pia raised her glass. He smiled.

A woman from behind the bar approached and handed him a sheet of paper. While he studied it, I studied him. He was the epitome of my type. Rock solid and muscular, maybe a little too much so, but I certainly wouldn't complain.

He wore a white dress shirt, with two buttons open at the collar, showing off his chest. His hair was dark brown, but from where I stood, his eyes looked more hazelnut. He had stubble on his chin, but not much. If my former best friends were here, they'd tease me about how I always went for the baby-faced-looking guys.

The bittersweet thought broke me out of my reverie. I looked back at my wine and then up at Pia.

"I know that look," she murmured. "A happy memory that turns sad." The expression on her face mirrored my own, then broke into a full-blown smile. "More wine!" she exclaimed, refilling my glass. "I think he should join us in the VIP room, *sì*?"

I took another sip of the Brunello. "It's your winery."

Pia rushed out, took the man's arm, and led him into the smaller room. She pulled another glass from the bar area and poured him some of the wine we were tasting.

"Why, thank you," he said, raising it to her.

"This is Valentini's Brunello di Montalcino. My friend Catarina says it's *fantastico*. What do you think?"

"I would agree," he said, taking a sip. His eyes met mine, and he smiled. While at first glance he looked Italian, his accent, I decided, was British, but every so often, he sounded more American. I couldn't place it.

"I am Pia Deltetto, and this is Catarina Benedetto. What is your name?"

"Ben Knox." He held his hand out to Pia, and she shook it. "Thank you again for the wine."

"You're welcome," she said, winking in my direction.

He turned to me. "It's very nice to meet you. Did you say your name was Catarina?"

"I did." I shook his hand and then pulled mine back when he hung on a little longer than necessary.

"Are you American?" he asked, raising his glass but keeping his eyes on me. "Such an Italian-sounding name."

"My parents love Italy." It wasn't a lie; they'd honeymooned here.

"It's a very beautiful name."

"Wait. Did you say you are Ben Knox?" asked Pia.

"That's right."

"You are staying in *la cascina.*"

"Yes."

"It's so nice to finally meet you in person. You have been here two days, *sì?*"

"That's right."

I noticed the tour guide walk into the tasting room. The others in the group did as well and began cashing out. "Looks like we're leaving."

"No! Not yet!" exclaimed Pia. "Where are you staying? In Pienza?"

"Um, most likely. I haven't quite figured that out yet."

"You could stay here."

"What do you mean?"

"We have accommodations. Much nicer than the *pensiones* in the village. Not that there's anything wrong with them. But what we have is better."

"Um…if you're sure."

"Of course I'm sure. Now, more wine, *sì*?"

7

Halo

Catarina Benedetto, aka Tara Emsworth, was far more beautiful than she appeared in her photos, and in those, she was still the prettiest woman I'd ever seen.

She had a broad smile that lit up her whole face, high angular cheekbones, and stunning deep blue eyes. Her blonde hair, even tied back, hung down almost to her waist, and her bangs fell just over her eyebrows.

When the woman—Pia—led me into the room, I was stunned almost speechless. In fact, I was certain my eyes were playing tricks on me. Could it really be that the woman I'd been looking for was truly sitting in this very room? It seemed inconceivable.

She turned skittish when I asked if she was American, and I immediately regretted doing so. Thankfully, Pia quickly changed the subject.

While *Catarina* informed the tour guide that she would not be returning to Sienna with them, Pia stepped out of the room to make a call. Not knowing how much time I had, I quickly fired off a text to Striker.

Tara Emsworth located in Val d'Orcia.

Copy that, came his quick response, followed by, *Details?* I put my phone in my pocket when Pia returned.

"I've asked Nonna Bella to arrange for some food to be brought to the winery. Did you have plans this evening?" she asked.

"None at all."

"I wonder where Catarina is," she murmured, looking out the window. "I hope she did not leave."

"Why would you think she would?"

She studied me as if I somehow held the answer. "I don't know." Pia tapped her cheek with her finger. "I'm going to go and check on her."

I took the opportunity to fire off another text to Striker. *Turned up at Valentini.*

Interesting.

I took a seat at one of the tables in the smaller room, hoping Tara would return to the tasting room before Pia did.

"Pia went looking for you," I told her when she did.

"Yes, um, I saw her."

"Are you staying?"

"The tour bus left, so I suppose it's that or try to find another way back to Sienna." She looked over her shoulder several times.

"Everything okay?"

"What? Yes. Everything's fine."

I was delighted when she took the seat across from me, only so I could look at her, study her, stare at her.

When Pia returned, she was carrying a platter. "This is Nonna Bella's white bean and prosciutto bruschetta," she said, setting it on the table. It looked fantastic.

We were served two more courses, and with each, Pia refilled our glasses. The wine had loosened Tara up, and while the haunted look in her eyes never went away entirely, she laughed easily and was animated in our conversations.

At one point, she stiffened when something outside caught her eye. Pia noticed it too and looked to see what it was.

"That is Georgio," she grumbled. "He is our winemaker."

"You sound as though you aren't happy he is," I commented.

Pia sighed. "I've known Georgio all my life. We were childhood playmates, but..."

"But what?" asked Tara.

"We are no longer friends."

I looked outside and saw the man on his phone, looking this way. Tara excused herself from the table and went to the lavatory.

Her instincts were telling her she was being watched. While Georgio definitely appeared to be up to something, his target was Pia.

"I don't recall meeting him, but he looks familiar," I said to her. "What's his last name?"

"Rossi." She turned her head from the window and toward me. "What brings you to Italy?"

"Work," I answered. Not a lie.

"What do you do?"

"I'm a journalist." Definitely a lie, but that was my cover.

She raised a brow. "A journalist? Interesting. I would've thought you would be…something in law enforcement perhaps."

I laughed. However, her assessment hit a little too close to home. "Why would you think that?"

She waved her hand in the direction of my chest. "You are…*molto muscoloso.*"

"I like to stay fit."

"Fit? You are more than fit. You could be…how do you call it…Mister Universe?"

Laughing again, I shook my head. "Not even close, but thank you."

She studied me. "Are you writing about Italy?"

"Yes."

"Is what you're writing about a secret?"

When Pia's face lit up, I turned to see Tara walking back to the table.

"Not secret," I said. "Just not necessarily very interesting."

"What is that?" Tara asked.

"Mr. Knox is a journalist. Surprising, I know. Because he is such *un uomo forte.* But anyway, he's writing about Italy."

Tara took in my body much like Pia had, not that I minded her eyes on me. "Broad subject matter."

"Yes, but as I said, my assignment isn't all that intriguing."

"Maybe you should find something more compelling to write about. Say, wine perhaps? Valentini's wines would make an excellent subject." Tara winked.

Pia leaned forward and put her elbows on the table. "Catarina, how do you know so much about our wine?"

She hesitated and her cheeks flushed. "It's been one of my favorites for some time."

"Do you remember where you first tasted it?"

"With some friends."

"I see." Pia was tapping her cheek with her finger.

"What?"

"It isn't just our wine you know a lot about."

Tara laughed. "Are you suggesting I drink too much wine?"

Pia laughed too, as did I.

"No, but I think you know more about Valentini wine than the others who work in the tasting room."

"I doubt that," Tara murmured.

"How long will you be in Italy?"

"I'm not certain. Indefinitely…for now."

While I appreciated the answers Pia was getting out of Tara without it seeming like an interrogation, I could see her growing increasingly uncomfortable.

"What will you be doing?" Pia continued her line of questioning.

Tara looked between her and me and bit her bottom lip. "I really don't know. Perhaps—"

Pia held up her hand. "I have a crazy idea," she said, getting up from the table. "I think you should work for us."

Tara's eyes opened wide. *"What?"*

"Sì."

"You can't be serious."

Pia sat back down and folded her arms. "I am very serious. You can stay here at Valentini too. We have many *casinas* you can choose from."

Tara looked at me and then back at Pia. "I would love that," she murmured, almost too softly to be heard.

Pia smiled and clapped her hands. *"Magnifico!"*

The tension I'd seen building in Tara vanished. "If I agree, you have to promise to tell me about Estancia Valentini. I've heard stories, but I'm sure they were greatly exaggerated."

"No, they are all true," said Pia, laughing. "My family has a very colorful history. Estancia was my seventh great-grandmother. She descended from the female line of the Medicis."

Tara turned to me. "Sounds like you may have found a compelling story to write."

We had far too much to drink, even with all the food Pia arranged to have delivered to the winery. When she noticed Tara yawning, she suggested she stay at the villa tonight, and tomorrow she'd get her settled in one of the small *casinas*.

I took the hint, stood, and said good night. "It was a pleasure meeting you both." I turned to our hostess. "Pia, thank you for your generosity."

"You are welcome." She smiled, looking between Tara and me.

"I hope to see you around Valentini, Catarina." Emboldened by the wine, I took her hand and brought it to my lips. *"Buona notte. Sogni d'oro."*

"Buona notte," she murmured in perfect Italian.

8

Tara

"He likes you," said Pia as we walked up to the villa.

"He's drunk."

She shook her head. "I watched him all night. He couldn't take his eyes off you."

"He was looking at you too."

Pia shook her head a second time. "Not the same way." She stopped when we got to the villa's *terrazza,* and looked out at the vineyards illuminated by moonlight. "I'm glad you are staying, Catarina."

"I am too. Thank you, Pia."

"I'm the one who should be thanking you. You have a great deal of knowledge about wine. Someday, you will tell me how you acquired it. But not tonight." She put her arm through mine and led me inside and up the stairs.

Something occurred to me. "Wait. I'm sorry. I can't work here."

"Why not?"

"I'm here as a tourist. I'd have to leave Italy to get a work visa." I couldn't tell Pia, but there was no way I could do that.

She shook her head. "Not to worry. We will pay you in cash. That will work, yes?"

It was the only thing that would work, actually. "Again, if you're certain."

"*Sì, naturalmente.* Now, come. You can stay in here tonight." She looked at my bag. "I didn't think to consider you wouldn't have your things."

"I don't have much, but you're right, I left them at the *pensione* in Sienna."

"We can make arrangements to collect them tomorrow." She tapped her cheek. "Hang on. I'll be right back."

When she was gone, I pulled out my phone like I did several times a day, hoping there'd be word from either my father or Brand. There wasn't.

"I know that look," Pia said, coming back to where I waited in the hallway, with towels and I guessed something for me to sleep in. "There are things that haunt you."

"Several, in fact," I mumbled, looking away from her.

"Me too." She sighed and took my hand. "I am happy you're here, Catarina. I think it's where you belong. At least for now. I can tell already that we will be friends."

I smiled. "Me too."

After she showed me to my room and said good night, I thought about how long it had been since I met anyone I felt such an immediate connection with. It wasn't since I was very young and met Pen, Ava, Aine, and Quinn.

After using the lavatory and changing into the night-shirt Pia had loaned me, I checked the burner phone one more time and snuggled into the most comfortable bed I'd slept in since I left America.

I woke the next morning to the sound of a knock at the door. It took me a minute to remember where I was. "Coming," I murmured.

When the door opened, I pulled the sheet up to my chin.

"Perdonami," said the young woman. "Didn't you say 'come in'?"

"It's fine. Um…can I help you?"

"I'm Lucia. Pia asked me to let you know breakfast is being served on the *terrazza*. She is there now."

"*Grazie.* Can you please tell her I'll be right down?"

Lucia backed out of the room and closed the door behind her. I got out of bed and looked out the window. From there, the vineyards that covered the hillsides were breathtaking. Every view I'd seen since arriving at Valentini was. It was so perfect, it looked like a film location.

My fingers itched to paint some of the Tuscan landscapes. How long had it been since I thought about painting? Maybe while I was in Sienna, picking up my things from the *pensione,* I'd look for a place where I could buy some art supplies.

Remembering Lucia had said Pia was waiting for me, I checked my phone and then quickly washed up and went downstairs where I found her having breakfast with the man we'd spent time talking to most of last evening.

"Good morning," he said, noticing me before Pia did.

"*Buongiorno,* Mr. Knox. Pia."

"Please, call me Ben." He stood to pull out a chair for me.

"Did you sleep well, Catarina?" Pia asked.

"Very well, thank you. Again, I appreciate your hospitality."

"You might not say that when you see how hard I'll make you work." Pia grasped my hand with hers and winked. "I'm just kidding."

Actually, the idea of work sounded so good to me. Admittedly, it was a feeling I'd rarely experienced before, and it shamed me.

"No! You are at Valentini. No more sad thoughts."

As much as her exclamation stunned me, her words did more. How was this woman I'd only met yesterday able to read me so easily? Was I really that transparent?

"Ben, what do you have planned today?" Pia asked.

"I have a meeting in Florence, and then I intend to visit Chianti."

I noticed he was drinking tea rather than coffee like Pia was.

"Are you British?" I asked, remembering that before he spoke yesterday, I'd been sure he was Italian because of his coloring and the way he carried himself.

"I'm more of a citizen of the world," he answered. "My father is American and my mother is Venezuelan.

We traveled around a lot when I was a kid, but spent much of my childhood in England."

"Is that where you live now?"

He shook his head. "We moved back to America when I was in high school."

That explained the difficulty I was having placing his accent. The fact that his mother was Venezuelan also explained why, initially, I believed him to be Italian. "What part?"

"Boston."

I loved the city and said so. "It's one of my favorites too."

I looked over at Pia; she was studying the two of us and smiling. "Perhaps you'd rather wait to start your new job tomorrow," she said, taking a bite of pastry. "You could visit Florence and Chianti with Ben."

"No," I said, perhaps too quickly. "Um, as nice as that sounds, I've been sightseeing quite a lot and am looking forward to learning more about Valentini."

"Perhaps another day," said Ben.

"Perhaps."

I stood and went to the buffet that had been set out on the *terrazza*. It all looked so good. Ben stood too, grabbed another plate, and piled it with fruit. "This will be my downfall," he said, pointing to the pastries before adding two to his plate.

"It doesn't appear it will be an issue," I said, not bothering to mask my perusal of his body. I smiled when his cheeks flushed. Mine did the same when he looked me up and down like I had him.

"For you either."

"Just to be safe, I think I'll stick with fruit. I'm still full from last night." When I turned around to return to the table, Pia was gone. "Where did she go?"

Ben shrugged. "I've no idea."

I set my plate on the table and poured myself a cup of coffee, added cream, and breathed in the aroma. It was heavenly. "What?" I asked when I sat down and noticed Ben staring at me.

"That sound…you made it a lot last night too."

"Sound?"

"You're very…expressive when you like something. It isn't just the murmurs of pleasure; your eyes roll back in your head a little." His voice was so soft and sexy I felt like I was falling into a trance.

"I'm sorry," I mumbled.

He leaned forward and rested his forearm on the table, almost close enough to touch. "Please don't apologize. I quite like it."

I looked away, unable to speak. It had been a long time since I had any real interest in a man. In fact, Pen had mentioned it a couple of times. "You might not be so bitchy if you got laid," she'd said on more than one occasion. A sad feeling, the one that washed over me whenever I thought about my friends, sat heavily on my chest.

"She's right, you know?"

That if I got laid, I wouldn't be so bitchy? Had I said that out loud? "I'm sorry, what?"

"You're at Valentini. No more sad memories." Ben repeated Pia's words from earlier.

"There's no switch to turn them off," I muttered, surprising even myself. I couldn't talk about the reasons I was sad, not to anyone, but especially not to a man from America.

He touched the back of my hand with his fingertip. "You're too beautiful to look so sad."

I looked into his eyes. "Thank you."

He sat back abruptly when Pia rejoined us. "Am I interrupting?" She smirked and then winked.

"I think we need to cheer Catarina up," said Ben.

I looked between them. "I'm fine."

Pia tapped her cheek. "I have an idea."

"Oh, no," I groaned under my breath, and she laughed.

"For you to be really good at your job in Valentini's tasting room, you should visit some of the other wineries in the area. That is the work you and I will do today. Since it is Monday, our tasting room and many others are closed. This will be the perfect time for us to visit."

"That doesn't sound much like work."

"It's research. We'll visit Chianti."

I stared at her with wide eyes.

"*Sì.*" She nodded. "That is what we will do." Pia looked at Ben. "And when your business is complete, you can join us."

"Pia!" I gasped.

"I'd like that very much," said Ben.

I looked between them again, incredulous. "I think you should give me a tour of Valentini instead today."

Pia nodded again. "We will do that this morning. This afternoon, we will go to Chianti. There are two wineries in particular we should visit. Casavetti, which is owned by my father's sister and her husband. The other, I'm not sure is a good idea."

"Which one?"

"Vitticio."

I'd heard of it and would certainly like to visit. "Why isn't it a good idea?"

"Paolo Vitticio." When she rolled her shoulders, the expression on her face changed drastically from a frown to a wide smile. "He is married now, so it will be fine."

I made a mental note to ask about him later when Pia and I were alone.

"It's a date, then, *sì*?" Pia looked at Ben.

"Yes. Absolutely." Ben looked at me.

"A date? Or work?" I asked.

"Both," answered Pia, grinning from ear to ear.

9

Halo

Given how late it was when I returned to the farm-house last night and the time difference, I waited until I'd finished breakfast to call Striker.

"You're sure it's her?" he asked.

I sent him a photo I'd taken of her and Pia last night. "See for yourself."

"Yep. That's her. What have you found out?"

"Not a lot." I told him about her arriving with a tour group yesterday and how one thing had led to another, resulting in Tara being offered a job at Valentini.

"A job?"

"That was my reaction."

"Interesting. Do you think she'll stay on?"

"I do. At least temporarily."

"This assignment might be over a hell of a lot quicker than we anticipated. My guess is her father is close by."

As much as I wanted to locate Richard Emsworth, I wasn't in any hurry for my time with Tara to end. Not that I'd admit it to Striker.

"I'll have the alerts K19 placed for Tara Emsworth pulled from the international agency wires. When you meet your AISE contact, advise him we've located the daughter and will continue surveilling her to see if she leads us to her father."

As much as I didn't want to ask, I had to. "Do you think she's aware of what her father was involved in?"

I heard Striker sigh. "Aine certainly doesn't believe so."

"Picking up cash in Switzerland doesn't look good."

"Her being in Italy doesn't look good either. Which reminds me McTiernan said that AISE believes her father has ties to the Calabrian crime syndicate."

This was not good news. The *'Ndrangheta* had been operating in the Calabria region of Italy since the eighteenth century. It was said that the organization's narcotics trafficking, extortion, and money laundering activities accounted for three percent of Italy's GDP. By some accounts, their annual income was fifty to sixty billion US dollars.

Like Sicily's Cosa Nostra, the 'Ndrangheta syndicate was comprised of approximately one hundred organized sub-groups, called *cosche,* each of which claimed sovereignty over a territory, usually a town or village. Within Calabria alone, it was estimated that there were six thousand members. Worldwide, that number doubled.

"Listen, Halo, if Tara is somehow involved, she's in way over her head. The Calabrians are considered to be the biggest cocaine smugglers in all of Europe. They aren't people to fuck with."

"Copy that."

The reason my base was in Tuscany, specifically at Valentini, was my AISE contact on the Emsworth investigation was none other than Mateo Casavetti, whose family's winery Pia had suggested we visit later today.

Pia, however, was completely unaware of who her cousin really worked for. Many agents employed by AISE worked undercover for the majority of their careers, given the level of corruption in Italy. To her, Mateo was the second son of her aunt and uncle, who worked at the winery along with his three brothers.

"We appreciate the support," said Agent Casavetti when I joined him at a field office in Florence. He led me into a meeting room where I was stunned to see a woman who worked for Valentini already seated at the table.

"This is Agent Lucia Cesare," he said when I raised a brow. "She asked to join us today to discuss the visitor who arrived at Valentini yesterday afternoon."

She stood, shook my hand, and sat back down.

"I'm assuming you're speaking of Tara Emsworth."

"She knows her father's whereabouts."

I looked between her and Mateo, who was seated beside her. "Is that right? Do you have proof she does?"

Lucia shook her head. "She should be brought in for questioning."

"That may be the way AISE would handle it, but I can assure you, it isn't the way I intend to."

"This isn't your jurisdiction."

"Excuse me?"

"This is an AISE investigation."

I looked at Mateo a second time. He hadn't said a word, and it was pissing me the fuck off.

"If that's what you think, this meeting is over."

Mateo's eyes opened wide. "What do you mean?"

"If you're under the impression I answer to you, you've been grossly misinformed. You don't want to do it my way, I'll go above your head. Way above. I'll have no problem continuing my investigation with or without AISE support."

When I stood, Mateo held up his hand. "There is no need for this. AISE is more than happy to do it your way."

"For now," I heard Lucia mutter under her breath.

What the fuck? I pulled out the brief and thumbed through it. There was no mention of Agent Cesare being assigned to work undercover at Valentini. In fact, there was no mention of her at all.

I set the brief aside, rested both hands on the conference table, and leaned forward. "Why wasn't I informed of Agent Cesare's involvement?" I asked the question of Mateo, but didn't take my eyes off Lucia.

"She is not working this investigation," he responded.

"Then, what is she doing at Valentini?"

"The reason is unrelated."

"The reason?"

"That Agent Cesare is undercover."

I shook my head. "It doesn't work that way. You tell me why she's there, or again, your involvement ends now."

"That information is classified."

Without another word, I picked up the brief, shoved it in my bag, and walked out. I knew, without question, that Doc would back me on this. There was no way I could be working this op from Valentini when another investigation was occurring simultaneously. That they hadn't shared anything about it, made it exponentially more dangerous for me.

I was almost to my car when I received a text from Mateo, telling me he'd received authorization to read me in.

"That's better," I muttered under my breath, turning to go back inside.

When I left thirty minutes later, I wasn't any less pissed off than I had been when I walked out. I was bypassing Striker, and I didn't give a fuck. Something was up, and my gut was telling me it was above my former boss' pay grade.

"Hey, Doc," I said when he answered my call.

"Halo."

"There's a situation with AISE I need to discuss with you."

"Go on."

I relayed the chain of events of my meeting with Agents Casavetti and Cesare.

"It isn't uncommon for AISE to have their heads up their asses."

"There's more." I told him what Mateo had shared with me about a string of accidents that had occurred at the Valentini winery over the course of the last few years, including one that almost killed Giovanni Deltetto, Pia's father. Five years ago, the man had been run over by a forklift and was left paralyzed. Two years later, he died of a heart attack.

"There were other accidents, Doc, but—"

"Why is AISE involved?"

"My thoughts exactly."

"Agent Casavetti wasn't forthcoming with the answer?"

"Negative."

"Let me see what I can find out."

"One other thing, the agent who's at Valentini undercover, Lucia Cesare, her father, who was the head winemaker there for many years, was also a victim of an accident that almost killed him."

"Another forklift?" Doc asked.

"Negative. This time, it was a faulty ventilation system. He suffered carbon dioxide poisoning."

I knew Doc was thinking the same thing I was. Neither of these accidents, nor the other minor ones the two agents had shared with me, were at a level that required AISE involvement. There had to be more to the story that neither Casavetti nor Cesare were willing to tell.

"I heard you found Tara."

"Yes, sir."

"While I realize there's a chance she may have played a role in the crimes her father is wanted for, I sincerely hope that isn't the case."

"Copy that, Doc."

Even more than for Striker, finding Tara had been personal for Doc. Long before K19 Security Solutions was in existence, Tara was Doc's daughter, Quinn's, best friend. While it was from a distance, he'd watched both women grow up.

Before getting on the road, I made one more call, to Tackle.

"How's Italy?" he asked.

"Every bit as beautiful as you would expect it to be."

"How come I don't get these assignments?"

That was a good question, one I didn't have an answer for. "I found Tara Emsworth," I said instead.

"Where?"

"Essentially under my nose."

I told him the same story I'd told Striker.

"That is unbelievable."

"I know."

My friend's tone changed. "What's going on, Knox?" he asked, using my first name rather than my code name, maybe recognizing the difference in my voice too.

"This is going to sound crazy."

"I'm listening."

"I know I'm way out of line here, but…she's…we connected. The second I saw her."

"It happens."

"It does?"

"Even when it isn't supposed to."

"So you know what I'm talking about?"

"Yep."

"What do I do?"

"You were with me on that plane, Knox. You know as well as I do that there's no way we should've survived that crash."

"Right."

"Live your life, my friend. Reach out and grab every bit of happiness you can."

"Is that what you're doing?"

"Damn straight, I am."

"The job—"

"Fuck the job."

When I walked into the tasting room at Casavetti, Pia and Tara were already there. "Good afternoon, ladies."

"Ben!" exclaimed Pia. "You made it." She tugged on Tara's arm. "Isn't that *fantastico*?"

Tara nodded, turned to me, mouthed, "Sorry," and rolled her eyes.

I looked her up and down. She looked as gorgeous today as she had yesterday. Instead of jeans and a sweater, she was wearing a tight-fitting charcoal-gray turtleneck with equally tight-fitting black pants. Instead of sandals, she wore mid-calf-height black boots.

"Do I look okay?" she asked when I got close enough that she could do so without anyone else hearing.

"You look beautiful."

Her cheeks flushed. "I wasn't fishing for a compliment. These clothes belong to Pia, and I'm quite a bit taller than she is."

"You look great," I said out loud, but inside, I wanted to tell her she looked so fucking sexy I could barely keep my hands off her. Tackle's words echoed in my head. "Reach out and grab every bit of happiness you can," he'd said. I leaned closer to her.

"Would you like to taste?" she asked, offering me her glass.

"If you don't mind sharing."

"It isn't my favorite," she whispered.

I took a sip of the white wine. "I would have to agree." When I reached around her and tossed what was left into the dump bucket, my body brushed against hers. She made the same mewling sound she had last night and this morning, and looked up at me. I stared into her deep blue eyes and then at her lush red lips, fighting an overwhelming desire to kiss her.

"Would you like to taste?" asked the woman behind the bar.

"We could share," Tara said before I had a chance to respond. "Since you're driving."

"I'd like that."

"What do you think of my cousin's wine?" Pia asked, jarring me out of the spell Tara had swept me under. I took an abrupt step back.

"It's very good," I said, clearing my throat. "Um, very good."

Pia swatted my arm. "You have no idea whether it is good or not. You're too busy admiring our Catarina."

"Guilty," I admitted, winking at Tara.

When we were finished in the tasting room, Pia gave us a tour of the Casavetti winery buildings. It seemed everywhere we went, we met another of her cousins. They all looked a lot like Mateo.

When we exited the last building, an older man approached. "Uncle Joe!" Pia exclaimed. "I want you to meet my friends. This is Catarina Benedetto and Ben Knox."

The man took Tara's hand and kissed the back of it.

"This is my uncle, Guiseppe Casavetti, but everyone calls him Joe."

"*Zia* Renata will want to see you and meet your friends, Pia. She's on the *terrazza*."

Pia cheek-kissed her uncle, and we followed her to the outside steps.

"Zia Renata is my father's sister," she explained. "She sometimes gets emotional when she sees me."

Evidently, this was not one of those times. Pia's aunt welcomed us graciously, immediately asking if we were hungry.

"I'm so sorry, Zia, but we're on our way to Vitticio. Perhaps another time."

"Vitticio?" she gasped.

"Yes, Zia. Catarina is working for Valentini, and we're visiting some of the other wineries' tasting rooms."

"But Vitticio?" her aunt asked. "*Paolo è cattivo*," she muttered under her breath.

"Zia, you exaggerate."

The woman shook her head.

"Do you understand what she said?" I whispered.

"She said that Paolo is wicked, evil. *Cattivo* means the same thing," Tara whispered back.

"Maybe we should skip Vitticio," I mumbled, although not quietly enough.

"*Sì*," said Pia's aunt. "We will eat instead."

10

Tara

"No, Zia. We cannot stay. If we don't go to Vitticio, we'll visit another winery," said Pia, hugging her aunt.

I wasn't sure why we couldn't stay, but I knew that even if we did, I wouldn't be able to eat another meal like I had the night before. I lost count of how many courses we'd gone through as well as how many bottles of wine.

My breath caught when Ben stepped closer, and his hand brushed mine. Earlier, if Pia hadn't interrupted us, I was sure he was going to kiss me. I was so disappointed when he took a step back. When I felt another brush of his hand, I looked down and then up into his eyes. I knew neither time had been accidental when he moved his hand again, took mine in his, and pulled our clasped hands behind his back. He stroked my thumb with his.

Pia was speaking to her aunt, but I was so focused on Ben, I couldn't hear anything she was saying.

He squeezed my hand and let go, stepping forward to say goodbye to Zia Renata.

"Are you okay?" Pia asked.

"Yes. Why do you ask?"

"You are so flushed. Do you have a fever?"

"I don't think so. Perhaps some water would be a good idea." I walked over to where I'd noticed a pitcher earlier and poured a glass.

"Everything all right?" Ben asked, standing close enough behind me that I could feel his warmth.

I couldn't stop myself. I leaned just slightly, so I could feel the muscles of his chest against my back. He moved his hand to my waist.

"That isn't helping," I whispered.

He leaned closer, so his mouth was next to my ear. "Are you sure?"

"I'm positive."

I turned my head just slightly, hoping Pia was still preoccupied with her conversation. She wasn't. She was looking right at us. Smiling.

"I have some business to take care of before we go to the next winery, and don't forget we need to go to Sienna to pick up your things from the *pensione*."

I'd completely forgotten about that, but Pia was right. It was something I had to do this afternoon.

"I could take Catarina to Sienna."

I looked up at Ben. "I don't want to trouble you."

"It's no trouble at all."

"Perfetto," squealed Pia. "We will meet in Pienza."

"Pienza? Is that where the other winery is?"

She shook her head and looked over her shoulder.

I laughed out loud. "What are you up to?"

Pia put her hand on her hip, but she didn't look angry. "Nothing!" She leaned forward and lowered her voice. "We will meet at *La Terrazza Del Chiostro*. It is owned by my friend Alejandra. That is where we'll have dinner."

I checked the time. It was early for dinner, but it would take us at least an hour to get to Sienna from here and then another hour from there to Pienza.

"This is me," said Ben when we reached the parking area. He held the passenger door of a sleek black car open for me.

"Thank you."

Before I could bend down to get in the car, Ben put his hand on my arm. "Wait."

I stood straight and stared into his eyes. "Look, I'm really embarrassed about the way Pia is pushing us together. If you'd prefer to go straight to Valentini, I understand, and I won't mind."

"That wasn't what I was going to say."

"Oh." I sighed and rolled my shoulders. "What were you going to say?"

"I would really like to…kiss you."

And I'd ruined it. I should just face the facts I really wasn't cut out for romance. Especially with someone like Ben—who was off-the-charts hot as fuck. When I bent down a second time to get in the car, he rested his hand on my shoulder.

"Catarina? Did you hear me? I said I'd really like to kiss you."

"Still?"

He smiled and nodded.

"I would like that too."

He leaned forward and touched my lips with his. His kiss was soft and sweet. When he ran his tongue over my lower lip, I opened to him and deepened the kiss. My fingers played with the soft curls at the base of his scalp, and I whimpered.

"I love that sound," he whispered, blowing into my ear before pulling back and looking into my eyes. "We should probably get going."

I bit my bottom lip. "Sure." I spun around and bent to get into the car, but he stopped me for the third time.

"There's a difference between not wanting to kiss you and feeling like I can't for other reasons." He wrapped his arm around my waist and pulled me into him.

"*Ciao!*" I heard Pia shout from across the parking area. "See you later in Pienza!"

Ben buried his head in my shoulder while I laughed and waved. "We should go."

"We should." When he didn't move, I gave him a push and got in the car.

When we arrived in Sienna, I offered to go into the *pensione* while Ben waited in the car. "I don't have much. It'll just be a minute," I'd told him, but he insisted on coming in with me.

"Please, allow me to be a gentleman."

Since I had everything already packed to leave, it only took us a minute to grab my bags from the room and be on our way.

"I'll just leave the key in the drop," I said as Ben went out to put my things in the car. When I followed a couple of minutes later, someone caught my eye from across the courtyard. A man ducked around the corner before I could get a good look at him, but from behind, I swear it could've been Brand.

I felt Ben's hand on my arm. "Everything okay?"

"Yes, fine," I said, turning to face him.

"You sure?"

When I nodded, he opened the car door, and I got in. Before he drove away, I took one more glance across the courtyard, but no one was there.

"You must be Ben and Catarina," a woman said when we approached *La Terrazza Del Chiostro*.

"We are," Ben answered. "Might you be Alejandra?"

"*Sì,* " she said, giggling when Ben kissed the back of her hand. "Pia asked me to tell you she's been delayed, but she will be here very soon."

My eyes met Ben's.

"Come," said Alejandra. "I have your table ready. Right this way."

I looked over my shoulder and smiled at Ben, who seemed to notice at the same time I did that the table was set for two people, not three.

"Pia is delayed. That is what you said?"

"*Sì,* she is only delayed."

"Delayed until tomorrow, I think," said Ben when Alejandra walked away. "I have to admit, I don't mind having you all to myself." He cleared his throat. "And probably better that we're in a public place."

He poured two glasses of wine from the bottle on the table and looked around for menus. I doubted we would need them. Like Pia the night before, Alejandra would probably continue bringing food until we couldn't eat another bite.

"So what brought you to Italy?" Ben asked.

I'd given the question a lot of thought, expecting it would come eventually. "The road less traveled," I murmured.

"What's that?"

"I needed a change. A big change. My life wasn't working the way it was."

He put his head in his hand and studied me.

"There have been times in my life when I thought a particular day was the worst ever. Maybe even that life as I knew it was over. In hindsight, I wonder if, instead, it was when my life really began." I had no idea why I was telling him all this. Why I decided this was the time to pour my heart out. "I'm sorry," I murmured. "More than you wanted to know."

He shook his head. "Not true. In fact, I could listen to you talk all night."

I rolled my eyes and laughed, but he didn't even crack a smile.

"I mean it, Catarina."

"What about you? You said you're a journalist?"

11

Halo

Tara had been as honest with me as she could be under the circumstances. She'd shared so much that I found myself wishing I didn't have to lie to her.

"The work I'm doing is investigative."

"Something to do with the Knights Templar?"

I was intrigued. "What makes you ask that particular question?"

"It's all the rage, isn't it? Buried treasures rumored to be left along Via Cassia. Can you imagine?"

I put my head in my hand, enthralled by this woman. I found myself wishing I really were a journalist. What fun Tara and I could have, exploring not just Tuscany, but all of Italy—writing about wine and "buried treasures" by day, ravishing one another's bodies by night.

"To be honest, I have more interest in the idea that they hid as much art as they did gold."

"A theory I've not heard."

She rested her elbow on the table and raised her hand just slightly. "I'll admit to being a bit of an art nerd. I have a degree in it, in fact. Well, the history of it."

I took a sip of wine, hoping she would continue. Instead, she looked lost in thought. "What made you choose art history?"

"Even when I was little, I could spend hours in galleries. It became an obsession, really." Her cheeks turned pink, and she bit her bottom lip. "So boring," she murmured, barely above a whisper. "What about you? Why journalism?"

We spent the next hour dancing around what we could and couldn't talk about. Only I was aware that's what we were doing. I still learned a lot about her without her needing to tell me about her family or her best friends.

I tried not to think about what I'd seen in Sienna, but I couldn't help it. I'd followed Tara's line of sight when she came out to the car, and saw a man duck around the corner. I caught enough of his height and build to know it couldn't have been Richard Emsworth, but who was it? It had shaken her enough I couldn't help but think she recognized him.

"Do you have any siblings?" she asked.

"I have a sister. Younger. Her name is Sloane."

"Are you close?"

"Not really." Saying the words out loud made me sad, especially after surviving the plane crash. Hadn't I vowed to tell the people who were important to me that I loved them? I'd certainly told Sloane, but had I done anything to forge a stronger relationship with her? "What about you?" I asked.

She shook her head. "No, but I always wished I did." She peered over her shoulder, stifling a yawn. "Would you mind if we went back to Valentini now? I don't even know where I'm sleeping tonight."

I knew where I wanted her to sleep. Although if she was in my bed, neither of us would get any rest. "Of course," I said, turning to look for Alejandra. When I didn't see her, I excused myself and asked one of the other servers to locate her.

"Can I bring you something?"

"No. I mean, yes. *Il conto per favore.*"

He shook his head. *"Non c'è fattura."*

"I insist, really."

"Scusa, but I have no bill."

The young man disappeared into the back, and I returned to our table.

"Let me guess; there is no bill."

I laughed. "You would be correct."

"It seems my new boss arranged not only for us to have a date, but also to take care of the check."

"I'd say she's more of a friend to you than a boss."

"I haven't known her much more than twenty-four hours."

I rested my hand on hers. "Sometimes that's all it takes."

"Are you suggesting that you, too, are my friend, Ben?"

"At the very least."

The drive from the village to Valentini was short. Tara was quiet the entire way. So much so, I wondered if she'd fallen asleep.

When we pulled through the gates, the lights were on in the villa. Instead of stopping at the farmhouse, which I would've much preferred to do, I drove straight up the hill.

"Thank you," Tara murmured when I parked near the *terrazza*.

"I'll walk with you."

Before we got to the front door, Lucia came outside. "Pia tried to reach you. There was an accident in the winery, and she was called away."

"Is everything okay?" Tara asked.

"She's at the hospital now, with the man who was injured."

"Is there anything we can do?" I asked.

"I don't think so."

"I'm sorry to ask, but did she mention anything about where I should stay tonight?"

Lucia shook her head at Tara's question. "She didn't."

"You can stay at the farmhouse," I told her. "There are three bedrooms. Plenty of room, and we can sort this all out in the morning."

She bit her bottom lip and looked into my eyes with her deep blue ones. "You're sure?"

Since Lucia was hanging on every word, I didn't tell Tara it would be my pleasure, although it very much would be. Even if nothing happened between us tonight, just having her stay with me at the farmhouse would make me happy.

"I left my bag…"

"I'll bring it to you," Lucia offered.

I wondered if the woman's rude treatment of Tara was due to my unpleasant exchange with her at our meeting earlier. One would think that the very least she could've done was place a call to Pia to ask if Tara should stay at the villa again tonight. Barring that, let the woman get her own belongings. The puzzled expression on Tara's face told me she was likely thinking the same things I was.

"Are you okay?" I asked when Lucia delivered the bag and I carried it to the car.

She nodded, but her expression didn't change. "I get the impression she doesn't like me very much."

"I'm sure Pia will be very unhappy at the way Lucia handled things."

"I don't want to cause trouble between Pia and the other employees."

I tried to appear casual when I put my arm around her shoulders and kissed her forehead, but all I felt was awkward. "You know what? It's been a long couple of days, far too much to eat and drink. We'll get a good night's sleep, and I'm sure by tomorrow, this won't seem like a big deal."

"Ben…I…"

"A good night's sleep, Catarina. That's all."

"You're sure?" she asked for the second time.

"Absolutely."

I would've much rather let Tara have the larger bedroom, but since my stuff was scattered all over, even taking her in there would've given her the wrong idea.

"The other bedrooms are smaller," I started to explain.

"I'm fine wherever. Honestly. I can sleep on the sofa."

"Definitely not necessary." I led her up the stairs to the first bedroom.

"Thanks for letting me stay here tonight."

"If there's anything you need, I'll be awake for a while. Just come down and look for me."

"Thank you," she repeated.

I let her be, went downstairs, and poured a glass of wine. It was a nice night, so I sat out on the *terrazza* and enjoyed the star-filled sky.

In the brief time since I found her, I'd crossed several lines with Tara. It would've been different if I was pretending to be attracted to her as part of the mission. Not that I'd ever resorted to that. I knew many agents operated that way, but I never had. No, the desire I had for Tara was completely genuine. Should I follow my best friend's advice, reach out, and grab every bit of happiness I could, even at what might be the expense of my job?

I looked over when I heard her come out the door from the kitchen.

"May I join you?" she asked.

"Of course." I held up my glass. "Want some?"

"No, thank you. I think I've had enough in the last couple of days."

I set my wine down on the table. I was guilty of the same.

"I couldn't sleep."

I wanted to ask what was worrying her, but the list of things she wouldn't be able to talk about was lengthy.

"I wanted you to know I'm planning on leaving tomorrow."

While that didn't surprise me, given Lucia's treatment of her, I was disappointed even more than concerned.

"It's none of my business…"

Tara smiled. "Go on."

"I haven't kept my attraction to you a secret, but that isn't the only reason I'd ask you to reconsider."

"What's the other reason?"

"As I said before, you might want to wait until you can talk to Pia in person."

"I wasn't going to leave by cover of night." She laughed, mesmerizing me.

"You have the most beguiling smile."

The moon was bright enough that I could see the flush that stained her cheeks.

"Thank you," she murmured.

I stood and held my hand out to her. Her eyes were questioning, but she took it and stood anyway. "Just in case," I whispered, putting my hand on the back of her neck. I leaned forward and kissed her in the same way I had earlier today when we were at Casavetti. The difference now was we didn't have an audience.

We didn't just kiss; I captured her mouth with mine, breathing in her erratic breath, plundering her lips and thrusting my tongue into her mouth.

She'd changed her clothes, taken off her bra, so I could feel the stiff peaks of her nipples against my chest. I kissed my way from her lips to her neck, wishing I could bend mine and suck one of the hardened tips into my mouth through the thin fabric of her nightshirt.

Tara's fingers wove into my hair, pulling it until my scalp tingled, taking my need for her from desperate to animalistic.

I cradled her ass, kneading and squeezing her flesh. In the back of my mind, I knew this was too much, but I couldn't stop. If I woke tomorrow or any other day and she was gone, I'd go to the ends of the earth to find her. In the meantime, I needed the memory of how her body felt next to mine to sustain me.

"Ben," she murmured.

"Tell me to stop, Catarina."

She didn't. She kissed me back harder and ground her body against mine. I tucked one hand into her thin pajama bottoms and grasped her hip to steady her.

"Be still," I groaned, bringing my mouth back to hers, if only to stop myself from clamping down hard on the nipples I couldn't wait to taste.

"Ben," she whimpered a second time. I longed to hear my name on her lips. The name I'd gone by all my life. *Knox.* I wanted to kiss her neck, mark it, claim her body under my real name, not the one I was using to keep her from knowing who I was, and not by a nickname I'd gotten in high school, even if it was my code name now.

When I came inside her, which I knew I would, I wanted to call out her real name. *Tara.*

I swept her into my arms and carried her inside. I stopped in the kitchen and set her on the large island. Without my asking, she lay back, her legs hanging off the edge with mine between them.

"Let me see you, baby."

Tara grabbed the hem of her thin shirt and pulled it up, exposing breasts I couldn't wait to get my hands and mouth on.

12

Tara

When I heard the knock on the door, I grabbed Ben's arm and pulled myself up with one hand while I pulled my shirt down with the other.

"Fucking hell," he muttered. "I'm sorry, but my guess is it's Pia."

"Go," I whispered. When he did, I jumped off the counter and rushed toward the door and out to the *terrazza*, if only to cool off.

I pulled out a chair and sat at the same time I heard Pia's voice. "I didn't interrupt anything, did I?" she asked Ben in a tone of voice that made me giggle.

"We were enjoying the nice night."

"Catarina?" Pia called out, standing in the doorway.

"I'm here." I waved as though she could see me and then pushed back my chair and walked toward her instead. I folded my arms in an effort to hide the fact I was dressed for bed.

"Mi dispiace," she said, taking a step back when I came inside. "I was worried when you weren't at the villa. Lucia told me she thought you might be here."

My eyes met Ben's. *Might be here?* Interesting. My resolve to leave tomorrow intensified. I couldn't risk working with someone who had it out for me. As much as I liked Pia and wanted to work here at Valentini, to do so would be foolish.

"It looks like you are ready to go to bed. We can talk in the morning," said Pia.

Here was my chance, and I had to take it. "Wait," I said when she turned to walk out of the kitchen. "About tomorrow…"

"Sì?"

"I appreciate your generous offer to work in the tasting room so much, but I think it would be best if I declined."

Pia looked from me to Ben and put her hands on her hips. *"Non capisco.* What happened?"

"Nothing happened. I just didn't plan on staying in Val d'Orcia."

Her eyes scrunched. "You are lying. Something happened that made you change your mind." Her gaze rested on Ben, who held up both hands.

"Don't look at me. I don't want her to leave any more than you do."

I sighed. "I don't want to take a job meant for someone else—"

"Who else? Did Georgio say something to you?" She sighed like I had. *"Il suo è un cane,"* she added under her breath.

"Georgio didn't say anything to me. Please, I don't want to upset anyone. My plan was always to return to Florence."

"Yesterday, you said you didn't have a plan. You were so excited." Pia shook her head. "If you think this is…how do you say? Charity? You are wrong. I have been looking for help in the tasting room and haven't found anyone with knowledge like yours."

"I find that hard to believe, Pia. You can't find anyone with knowledge about Italian wine?"

"Will you excuse us?" she said to Ben.

"Of course." He went out the door to the *terrazza* and closed it behind him.

"Can we sit?"

"Sure." I pulled out a chair at the table.

"Things have not been…easy for me since my papà died. My mamma has been ill, and the doctors have no idea what is wrong with her. Georgio, who used to be like a brother to me, argues and disrespects me. We have had many accidents, like the one earlier tonight."

"I'm sorry. I meant to ask. Is whoever was injured going to be okay?"

"*Sì,* but…I am not sure how to say this. I need someone in the winery who is on *my* side. Even if it is just in the tasting room."

"How can you be sure I'm that person? You don't even know me."

Pia tilted her head. "I am sure you've experienced what I have before. When you meet someone and immediately know that you will be friends?"

I had, and for many years, the four women I met in second grade had been my lifeline. They no longer were.

"Please stay, Catarina."

How could I say no? I could *feel* her pleading with me. "Okay."

Rather than her face breaking into an immediate smile like it had every other time I'd conceded something she asked, she remained serious.

"You must tell me what happened that made you reconsider."

"Again, nothing happened, Pia. I thought maybe your offer had been made in haste."

She sat back in the chair, her eyes scrunched again. "I know something happened. You will tell me eventually." She motioned with her head to the door that led outside. "You feel the same with Ben, *sì*?"

"That we'll be friends?"

Pia smiled for the first time since we began talking. "Friends? I think perhaps more than that."

I shrugged one shoulder.

She stood and patted my hand. "Tomorrow, I will tell you a story about my *friend,* Mylos. Tonight, I'll leave you and Ben to get to know each other better."

"Could we also figure out where I'll be staying tomorrow?"

Pia smiled again and raised a brow. "If you still need to."

I smiled too and shook my head.

Once Pia left, I went outside and joined Ben on the *terrazza.*

"How did it go?" he asked.

"Fine. She's impossible to say no to."

He held his hand out to me, but instead of taking it, I sat in the chair beside him. Ben leaned forward and rested his arms on the table. "You're cold," he said, noticing I rubbed the chill bumps on my arms. "Let's go inside."

When I pulled the chair out in the kitchen to sit where I had been when I talked with Pia, Ben took my hand and pulled me into the other room. He motioned for me to sit on the sofa and sat beside me.

"I'm happy you're staying."

I smiled. "Me too."

"When I thought about you leaving, I knew I had to kiss you. I may have gotten carried away, but, Catarina, there has been an intense attraction between us since the moment we met. For me anyway. I sense you feel the same."

"You know I do," I said, embarrassment flushing my cheeks.

"It's been a long day, following an equally long one. We both need rest."

When I stood, Ben grasped my hand with his. "I want to kiss you, but if I do, I fear I'll get carried away again."

"I fear it too." I pulled my hand from his and walked over to the staircase. "Good night, Ben."

I traipsed up the stairs, wishing he had kissed me again, wishing I'd kissed him. If I had, I'd be in his arms right now—the place I longed to be.

Attending both an all-girls boarding school and college didn't preclude me from dating, but it didn't make it any easier. Coupled with the fact that in my tribe of five, one of us was more beautiful than the next, which meant I wasn't often the one guys went for. Admittedly, I was a bit standoffish, something Penelope had called me out on numerous times.

"If you weren't such a bitch to them, more guys would ask you out," she'd said one night after we both had too much to drink. I called her a few choice names back, and the evening ended with neither of us speaking to each other. It all seemed so trivial now, when I missed her, Ava, Aine, and Quinn so much it sometimes felt hard to breathe.

Had I been a bitch to Ben? If it had been Pen with him instead of me, she would've had sex with him without giving it a second thought. She also would have no intention of seeing him again, and if she had, she would've played it off like it was no big deal. I couldn't do that.

I was in bed, tossing and turning, when I heard his footsteps on the stairs. When they stopped outside my door, I held my breath, willing him to come in. After several seconds, he continued down the hallway.

The next morning, when I went downstairs, I found a note from Ben in the kitchen. It said he'd had to leave for a couple of days, something about the article he was writing, but hoped to see me when he returned later in the week.

I was disappointed, of course, especially considering he hadn't mentioned he'd be leaving last night. It was for the best, though. I needed to focus on my new job in the tasting room. If Ben were around, not only would I be distracted, but Pia would continue to push the two of us together.

Not knowing what else to do, I walked up to the winery, hoping I'd find Pia in the office.

"Buongiorno," she said, coming to the door when I knocked.

"Buongiorno."

"Did you sleep well, Catarina?"

"I did," I lied. "Um, I was hoping I could start in the tasting room today. That's if you still need someone."

Pia laughed, grabbed my arm, and pulled me inside. "If I still need someone? It was only last night I begged you to stay. Did you think that would change with the dawn of a new day?"

I shook my head. "I just want you to know I appreciate this."

"Come," she said, pulling me back outside by the hand. "You and I will work in the tasting room together today."

By the end of the second day, I was exhausted. My feet hurt, and I had a headache, but I couldn't remember another time in my life when I'd been as happy, even in my discomfort. Pia told me time and again that she and I made a great team. She also said wine sales were triple what they'd been in the week prior.

"You're so passionate. People are leaving with cases of the vintages you recommend."

It wasn't difficult to talk about Valentini wine; I loved it. Sharing the nuances of each vintage was something I could do all day—and had.

Like she had last evening, Pia invited me to join her for dinner, but I begged off. I walked to the *casina* she'd put me up in and opened the door. I sat down on the two-seat *divano,* took off my shoes, and rubbed my feet. I tucked my legs under me and rested my head against the arm.

I'd been too busy during the day to think about Ben and too tired at night. Now, though, I wondered again about his abrupt departure. Was it because I'd essentially turned him down? He could rest easy when he returned, I supposed, since I had a place of my own now. I let my eyes drift closed, remembering how good his kisses felt, how much I loved having his hands on me.

When I heard a knock, I sat up, disoriented. I must've dozed off. I checked the time, stunned to see two hours had passed.

When I heard a second knock, I got up and opened the door.

"Hi," said Ben, leaning against the doorjamb.

"Hi," I answered, stifling a yawn.

"Bad time?"

"I took an unintentional nap."

When he didn't say anything, it occurred to me he was waiting for me to ask him in. I stepped to the side and waved my hand.

"Am I intruding?"

"No." I bit my bottom lip.

"It appears I might be."

"It isn't that."

"What is it, then?"

If I told him I didn't like the way he'd left after I spent the night at the farmhouse, would I sound like a shrew? "I don't have anything to offer you except water," I said instead.

"I've actually come to invite you to dinner."

"Oh…um…" I looked over at my one and only pair of shoes nice enough to wear to work that was tucked under the *divano*. I cringed at the thought of putting them back on.

I looked back at Ben, struck like I had been the first time we met by how handsome he was. His hazelnut eyes were so warm, and his smile so sweet. All I wanted to do was fall into his strong arms and rest my head against the broad expanse of his muscular chest. My gaze rested on his lips. Kissing him again would be quite nice too.

He took a step closer. "You're tired." He reached up and brushed my hair from my face.

I desperately needed to get it cut; my bangs had been in my eyes all day.

"I should go," he murmured.

I clasped his hand and brought it to my face. When he cupped my cheek, I leaned into his palm.

"Maybe not."

"Definitely not." I sighed. "Except if you're hungry or thirsty, in which case, you've come to the wrong place."

Ben wrapped his other arm around my waist. "I'm starving, Catarina, and I've come to exactly the right place." With his hand still cupping my cheek, he leaned forward and kissed me.

I groaned when he thrust his tongue into my mouth. Had any other kiss I'd ever had felt as right as this one did? Instead of being awkward, it was as though our mouths were a perfect fit. It wasn't just our mouths; our bodies fit too.

"God, I like kissing you." Ben rested his forehead against mine.

I looked around the *casina*. Other than the two-seat *divano*, which wasn't all that comfortable even for one person, the only other place we could sit next to each other was at the dining table or on the bed.

"Tell you what. Since you said you don't have any-thing to eat or drink here, how about we go down to the farmhouse and I'll make us dinner."

"You don't have to do that."

"And if I want to?"

"That sounds nice." I looked back over at my shoes, wishing I could just stay barefoot.

"What?"

What would Ben say if I admitted my feet hurt from being on them for two days straight? Would it give him a glimpse of the entitled, spoiled brat I'd been all my life?

He took a step closer and cupped my cheek with his palm. "There it is again."

I looked into his eyes.

"I wish I had the power to take away the memories that haunt you. Replace them with happy ones."

"Maybe you do," I murmured, wishing as soon as I had that I hadn't.

"I'd like to believe I can."

"Ben, I…"

He kissed me, perhaps knowing it was the only thing that would soothe me. "If I'm ever the cause of your sadness, I want you to tell me."

13

Halo

Tara took a step back and turned away from me, but I could see that she bit her lower lip.

"Ah, so I am the cause."

"Not entirely," she mumbled.

It wasn't long after Tara had gone upstairs two nights ago that I got a message from Striker, asking me to check in. When I told him what I'd witnessed when we were in Sienna, he suggested I lay low for a few days and see if anyone showed up at Valentini or followed Tara if she went back to the *pensione*.

I thought about knocking on her door when I went up to bed to tell her I had to leave for a few days, but if she was asleep, I didn't want to wake her.

I'd kept a distant watch for almost forty-eight hours before deciding it was a waste of time. No one resembling the man I'd seen in Sienna came into the tasting room either day while she was there and, certainly, no one she'd had such a strong reaction to.

Last night, after she had dinner with Pia and her mother on the villa's *terrazza,* I'd watched from a distance as she walked back to the *casina* where she and Pia had taken her things earlier in the day. Less than twenty minutes later, the lights were off, and I was sure she was asleep.

When she walked back to the *casina* earlier tonight, I made the decision to drive into town and pick up some groceries. I came straight here when I returned.

How could I explain it to her now in a way that sounded at all plausible? "I told you the other night that my work is investigative," I began.

She stiffened and kept her back to me. *Wrong tack.* I was, in essence, holding up a red flag, and that wasn't what I wanted to do.

"Catarina?"

"Yes?"

"Please look at me."

She turned partway.

"I received a message after you went to bed about a lead on a story that I needed to follow up on."

"You don't owe me an explanation."

"No? Yet I contributed to your sadness."

"It's fine."

"Uh-oh."

Her eyes opened wide. "What?"

"Whenever my mother told my father that everything was fine, my sister and I knew it was anything but."

Tara smiled, and I couldn't stand it a moment longer. I pulled her back into my arms. "It's very difficult for me to be around you and not kiss you, not touch you."

"I feel the same way." Tara finally looked into my eyes.

"So, what about going to the farmhouse?"

"I need to change my clothes."

"If you're tired, I could help."

That got another smile out of her. However, not from me since she didn't take me up on it.

"You have your car," she said when we walked outside.

"I was in a hurry to see you."

She smiled a third time, and as much as it made me want to kiss her, I wanted to get us to the farmhouse more. That way, when I did bring my lips to hers, I wouldn't have to think about stopping.

The only thing I didn't consider is how I would explain why I hadn't offered to bring the groceries I'd picked up on my way back to Valentini into her *casina* and make dinner for her there.

When I parked and went to fetch the bags, she offered to help, but otherwise, didn't say anything.

"What can I do?" she asked as I unloaded the bags.

"Are you interested in wine, or are you getting tired of it?"

"I'd love some," she said, walking over to where several bottles were stored. I watched as she studied them. "Oh, you have a Biondi Santi." She pulled the bottle out and held it up. "Would you mind?"

"Not at all. A favorite of yours?"

"I've never tried it, but I've been dying to. It's said that the family invented Brunello."

"How does one invent a wine?"

"Well," she said, pouring two glasses after she opened the bottle. "The story goes that in the mid-nineteenth century, a local farmer, named Santi, nurtured a certain vineyard where he planted Sangiovese vines in a way he hadn't any other. The soil, the sun, the rain—he believed—were as perfect a combination as there could ever be. He made wine from that vineyard only and aged it for several years. When Santi was given the opportunity to share it with the prime minister of Tuscany, the man declared it the best in all of Italy."

She swirled the wine and inhaled, whimpering in that way I loved. Her eyes rolled back in her head, and I smiled.

"Santi named it Brunello, and since his vineyards were in the Montalcino region, Brunello di Montalcino was born."

"Did you learn all that from Pia? That's the wine they make, right?"

She took another sip. "Yes, and no. Or no, and yes."

I cocked my head.

"No, I didn't learn that from Pia, and yes, Valentini is known for their Brunello di Montalcino."

"She wasn't exaggerating when she said you know a lot about wine."

"Wine and art," she muttered. "I'm an expert in useless information," she added under her breath.

I set down the knife I was using to chop vegetables for our dinner and walked over to her. "Not useless," I said, putting my arms around her waist. "Pia picked up on that right away." I leaned forward and kissed her. I couldn't help it. When she was in my arms, I was powerless not to. I touched the tip of her nose with my finger. "If I keep kissing you, we'll never eat."

"I have to admit, I am hungrier than I thought I'd be. I was so exhausted when I got back to the *casina* tonight."

"Long day?" I asked, washing my hands and tossing the vegetables into the olive oil heating in the pan.

"Tiring, but in a good way."

Tara told me how she and Pia had worked the tasting room together today and yesterday and how their sales were triple what they were the week before.

"She said we are a good team."

"I would have to agree. The two of you seemed to hit it off right off the bat."

The haunted look in her eyes was fleeting, but I saw it and wished I'd kept my mouth shut.

"What about tomorrow? Are the two of you working together again?"

She took a drink of her wine and shook her head. "I'm off tomorrow since I'm working all weekend."

"Any idea what you'll do?"

"I'm going into Florence."

"For?"

"Sto visitando il Museo Nazionale di San Marco," she said in flawless Italian.

"That was so fucking sexy," I murmured, resting both my hands on the kitchen island where just two nights ago, she'd been spread out, showing me her tits.

Tara smiled and came around to where I was cooking. "Um, I think you might want to turn the heat down a little."

Heat? Down? What did she say? I looked at the pan in front of me and at the edges of the vegetables that were turning black. "Oh. Right." I turned the burner off.

She laughed. "What just happened?"

"Flashbacks," I said, pointing to the counter with my spatula.

"Yeah?" she asked, looking down at where my rock-hard cock strained my zipper.

"Sorry," I mumbled.

"Tell you what. You give me a taste, and I'll reciprocate."

I looked up at her, and she motioned with her head to the pan. "A mushroom, please."

I grabbed a fork, speared one, and brought it to her mouth.

"Mmm. That tastes so good. Your turn. What do you want to try?"

Was she really saying what I thought she was? Unable to speak, I motioned to her tits with the fork.

"This?" she asked, pointing where I had.

I nodded. Maybe I grunted. I know I groaned when she pulled her shirt over her head and I saw her breasts were bare beneath it.

I put one arm around her back and leaned forward, getting as much of her tit in my mouth as I could. I swirled my tongue around her nipple. Tara weaved her fingers in my hair, and when I went to move to the other breast, she pulled.

"Uh-uh. My turn."

I stood and, since I'd suddenly gone mute, pointed at the pan of veggies.

"A pepper, please."

I speared it and brought it to her mouth. She chewed it slowly, making the same sound she had when she tasted the wine. Her eyes, instead of rolling back in her head, stayed fixed on mine.

She motioned with her hands to her boobs, but I had a different idea. Instead of going for seconds, I brought my lips to her mouth.

"Oh my God," I moaned, finally finding my voice. "You taste so…damn…good." I cupped her face with both my hands and pressed against her lips with my tongue, thrusting inside when she opened to me. When I angled my head and went deeper, Tara wrapped her arms around my neck.

I reached down and put both hands on her ass, lifting until her legs went around my waist.

"What do you want a taste of now, baby?"

She plastered her mouth against mine and kissed me as hard as I'd kissed her. After a few moments of dueling tongues, I pulled back. "Does this mean it's my turn again?"

"Mm-hmm."

I carried her around the counter and set her on her ass where I had the other night. Just like then, she leaned back, resting against the cool stone. I unfastened the button on her jeans and lowered the zipper.

Since it was my turn, and I knew what I wanted to taste, I pulled her jeans and panties over her curves, and down until they fell to the floor.

"Put your feet here," I said, lifting one and then the other so they rested on the edge of the counter. "Drop your knees."

Tara was spread out before me, and I intended not just to taste, but to eat my fill.

When I ran my tongue through her moist folds, she whimpered. I reached up with one hand and pinched the nipple I'd had a taste of. I'd get back to the other one soon.

I drank in her wetness and gently inserted one finger into her pussy. Tara's back arched, and she wove her fingers in my hair. She could pull all she wanted, but I had no intention of breaking the seal my lips had on her sex.

I added a second finger and brushed her clit with the pad of my thumb. A groan built deep in her chest, slowly working its way up her neck until it came out of her mouth in a scream. I sucked in everything she gave me, grasping her hips with both hands to keep her from writhing away from my mouth.

"I'm not finished," I murmured when she tried to twist away.

"I can't…" she whined.

"Wanna bet?" I dove back in, licking while my fingers continued their assault on every part of her perfect pussy. Her hands pulled at my hair, but my sense of taste and smell overpowered any feeling of pain.

"Come on, Catarina. Give it to me again."

Instead of another scream, this time, she cried out her pleasure. The build was slower, but the wetness on my lips was no less voluminous.

I kissed my way up her body, stopping to taste the nipple she'd deprived me of earlier. I remained there, going back and forth between both breasts until I felt the tension in her body ease.

I looked up, and her eyes were open, studying me. "Your turn," I said with a grin.

14

Tara

Ben held his hand out to help me sit up. The stone counter felt ice cold on my overheated pussy, and I wiggled.

"Here," he said, handing me my panties, but I didn't want them. I shook my head and pushed him back so I could stand. He turned to walk away, and I grabbed the belt loop on the back of his pants. He peered over his shoulder and smiled. "No more veggies?"

"Not now."

He took a drink of wine and rested against the counter. I put my hands on the waist of his jeans and sunk to my knees in front of him, easing open his zipper and gasping when I realized he wore nothing under them.

He grabbed my wrists before I could lower them any farther. "Catarina…"

I wriggled from his grasp.

"Let me," I whispered, wanting to bring him the same kind of pleasure he'd brought me. The idea that, earlier, just imagining me spread out for him had distracted him, excited him, enough that he couldn't focus, emboldened me to offer my challenge of tastes.

"Ben," I half whimpered when his cock sprung from the confines of his jeans.

He moaned when I touched the tip with my tongue. I looked up as I continued to swirl around him. "Catarina…" he said, his voice straining.

If he said anything else, I didn't hear him. I was just as lost in my desire to make him lose himself too.

"Jesus," he groaned, holding the sides of my head as he came in my mouth. "Come here." He pulled me to my feet and held me close to him. He put his fingers on my chin and brought his lips to my neck. "My turn," he murmured, licking a trail to right below my ear.

When chill bumps covered my body, he wrapped me tighter in his arms, laughing that we were both naked but for the shirt that covered the top half of him.

When I reached for my top, he took it from my hand and helped me put it back over my head, then handed me my panties. At the same time he pulled on his pants, I heard a cell phone.

"Not mine," he said when my eyes met his.

I rushed over and pulled mine out of my bag. It wasn't a number I recognized, but it had to be either my dad or Brand calling. "Excuse me," I muttered, rushing out the door to the *terrazza.* "Brand?" I whispered.

"Hello, *passerotta.*"

"Thank God," I muttered, looking over my shoulder to make sure Ben hadn't followed me out. "Where are you? I've been so worried."

"I'm here. Where are you?"

"At Valentini."

"Yes, sweetheart, I'm aware. Where specifically?"

I told him I was at the farmhouse.

"I can't stay long—"

"Wait. When you said here, you meant at Valentini?"

"You're catching on."

"I'll be right there."

I had no idea how I'd explain to Ben why I had to leave so abruptly. I couldn't lie and say Pia needed me. What if he ran into her and asked?

"Everything okay?" he asked when I went inside.

"I'm sorry, but I need to cut our evening short. I, um, have some things I have to take care of."

He walked over and cupped my cheek. "Anything I can help with?"

I took a step back. "No, but I appreciate the offer." I put my phone in my bag and slung it over my shoulder.

"Oh, you mean you need to leave *now*? I thought we could at least finish dinner."

I nodded and apologized again. "I'll see you soon?" I said, heading for the door.

"You don't need to walk. I'll drive you up to the *casina*."

"That isn't necessary, really. Thanks. I'm fine walking." I doubted Brand would show his face, but I didn't want to risk it any more than him seeing Ben.

"Catarina?"

I was about to slip out the front door. "Yes?"

"Are you okay?"

"Yes. I'm fine." I knew my cheeks were flushed, but I didn't have time to try to come up with a lie to explain why I was acting this way. "Bye, Ben."

I rushed out and closed the door behind me, hoping he wouldn't follow. I felt terrible, but I had no choice but to leave the way I had. I raced through the vineyards and up the hillside. When I walked into the *casina*, I saw Brand standing in the bedroom doorway.

"I've been so worried," I cried, running into his embrace.

Brand stroked my hair and kissed my forehead. "It's okay, *passerotta*."

Brand's nickname for me, which translated to "little sparrow," was an Italian term of endearment for anyone metaphorically "learning to fly." I couldn't remember when he'd started referring to me that way, but I loved it.

"Come," he said, pulling me into the bedroom. "You've been a very bad girl, Tara," he said, his expression darkening.

"What do you mean?"

"I told you we needed to talk when you returned to New York. Instead, you're here."

"But my dad—"

Brand put his fingers on my lips. "You need to go home, Tara. Now. If not tonight, tomorrow."

15

Halo

When she went out the front door of the farmhouse, I followed out the back, keeping far enough away that she wouldn't hear me, but close enough that I could see her. I'd anticipated there would be someone waiting for her at the *casina*, but not my reaction to seeing it was a man close to my own age—particularly one she looked so happy to see.

I clenched my fists when I saw the man put his arms around her, but when I saw them go into the bedroom, it was all I could do not to break the fucking door down and put him through a wall.

I crept around to the other side of the structure so I could see in the window of the other room and watched as they sat on the edge of the bed and talked. I wanted to rip his arms off when I saw him touch her.

I took out my phone and captured several photos, hoping I'd get at least one that would allow someone from K19 to identify the man.

They stood and turned off the light in the bedroom, so I crept back around to the other side of the *casina*. I got there just in time to catch the end of their embrace. When the man brushed her cheek with the back of his hand, I assumed it was because she was crying.

In what felt like a mixture of sorrow and trepidation, I watched as she flung herself back into his arms. I looked away, knowing that if she kissed him, I wouldn't be able to stand it.

The front door creaked, and the man stepped outside. "I'll see you tomorrow in Florence, *passerotta,*" he said, shaking a finger at her. "Do not forget what I told you."

Florence. That's where she said she was going tomorrow, evidently to meet up with this man. I could say one thing with absolute certainty. I was headed to Florence tomorrow too.

When I returned to the farmhouse, I called Striker, but he didn't pick up. Wanting answers as soon as I could get them, I called Doc directly.

"Halo," he said when he answered the call. "I was about to send you an email."

"About?"

"I haven't been able to find anything on AISE's investigation into the accidents at Valentini, but wanted you to know I'm still working on it."

"Copy that."

"Why'd you call me?"

I told him about the scene I'd just witnessed up at the *casina*.

"Any idea who the guy is?"

"Negative, but I've got images."

"Send 'em over, and I'll work it on our end. It may be a day or two before you hear back from me."

"Copy that. Thanks, Doc."

When the call ended, I threw my phone on the sofa, the same one I'd sat on with Tara only a couple of nights ago. Imagining her there made me sick to my stomach. Worse would be going into the kitchen, where our half-prepared dinner still sat. There was no way I could deal with that shit tonight. I picked up my phone and went upstairs, knowing I wouldn't be getting a moment's sleep tonight.

When I saw the sun on the horizon, I took a shower and went back to one of the places I'd used to surveil Tara's *casina* when she thought I was away.

Two hours later, she came out the front door and walked in the direction of the villa. I followed, and when I saw her join Pia on the *terrazza* for breakfast, I did the same. As a guest staying at the farmhouse, it was something I'd been invited to do during my stay.

"Good morning, ladies," I said, walking over to make a cup of tea.

"*Buongiorno,* Ben," said Pia, looking from me to Tara, who stood and approached me.

"Good morning," she murmured, a soft smile on her face. "I'm sorry about having to leave so abruptly last night."

Interesting. If this was how she was going to play it, I could play along. I leaned forward so my mouth was close to her ear. "I'm looking forward to picking up where we left off."

Not only did her cheeks flush, but her nipples hardened. "I'd like that," I heard her whisper.

Inside, a war was waging, but on the surface, I kept it together. "Still heading to Florence today?"

"I am."

I couldn't wait to see how she'd handle this. "Up for some company?"

"Do you have time?" she asked, stunning me.

"I've got all day. Night too," I added with a wink.

"Do you think it would be a problem if I brought someone with me?" she asked Pia, who picked her mobile up from the table.

"Let me check, but I don't think so."

"Pia was kind enough to make me a reservation at the Museo di San Marco," Tara explained.

"No problem to add another person," Pia said, setting her phone back down. "I'm so happy you'll be able to enjoy it together."

I decided to push harder. "Can you spare our Catarina tomorrow?"

Tara's eyes scrunched, and Pia smiled. "Take all the time you'd like. Our Catarina deserves some time off after all the wine she sold in the last two days."

"I thought I'd make a reservation at a *pensione*. That way, we could have dinner in Florence too."

"Um…sure…we can talk about it before we head out," said Tara. She turned her back to get more coffee, but I didn't miss that she bit her bottom lip.

"Is there something else you need to do while you're in Florence?"

She looked up at me and cocked her head. "No. Why do you ask?"

"You seem distracted."

"Not at all." She filled a plate with fruit and sat down at the table.

"What time is our reservation?"

"At one. You should leave soon," answered Pia.

Given it would take at least two hours to get to Florence from here, soon meant within the next thirty minutes. If I wanted to keep up the charade until Tara was forced to end it, I had to make her think I'd meant what I said about spending the night.

"Shall I help you grab your things, and then we can get mine from the farmhouse?"

"I won't need much. I'll just meet you down there."

Sure, that would give her time to call *Romeo* and alert him she wouldn't be visiting Florence alone. "I can walk with you."

Pia cleared her throat. "You go on, Catarina. I need to speak with Ben about something." She leveled her gaze at me and waited until Tara was at the bottom of the stairs before speaking again. "What is going on?"

"What do you mean?"

"Please, sit." She motioned to the chair beside her. "Catarina is too polite to rescind her invitation, but

I am not. You are speaking to her as though you are angry with her. Why?"

I could tell Pia it was none of her concern, but that certainly wouldn't serve me well.

"I don't know what you're talking about."

She leaned over and put her hand on my arm. "I'll admit I don't know very much about Catarina. However, over the two days we worked in the winery together, every time I mentioned your name, she smiled. Sometimes it quickly turned to sadness. It was then I wondered if something had gone wrong between the two of you."

"You're imagining things, Pia."

She sat back and folded her arms. "I am not imagining anything." She studied me. "If you hurt my friend, I will not be happy, Ben Knox."

If anything, it shouldn't be me she was warning.

"There she is," said Pia, pointing at Tara, who was walking in our direction, carrying the same small bag Lucia had brought out to her the other night. "She was looking forward to this, Ben. Please don't spoil it for her."

"I won't," I muttered, going down the steps so she wouldn't have to come all the way up to the *terrazza.* "Ready?"

"If you changed your mind, I'll understand," she said. I put my hand on her chin and pulled her lip from where she was biting it.

"Why would you say that?"

She shrugged.

"I do want to go. There was something on my mind, and I'm sorry if I gave you the impression I was angry with you. I'm not."

She nodded and folded her arms.

"There's one other thing." If she was really going to go through with this and stay the night in Florence, I didn't want her to think she had no choice but to share a room with me.

"What?" she asked.

"I can reserve two rooms at the *pensione.*"

"Is that what you want to do, Ben?"

Did I? When I looked into her eyes, no. When I thought about the man I'd seen her with, yes.

"I'm sorry I had to leave the way I did last night. It had nothing to do with you." It was the second time she apologized.

"I know." It took me a couple of seconds to notice Tara had stopped walking. "What?"

"You haven't accepted my apology."

"I didn't realize it was required."

"I've lost interest in going to the museum. You're welcome to still go."

"Because I didn't accept your apology?"

"Something changed, Ben. At first, I thought it was because I had to leave the way I did, but I said I was sorry. If that isn't good enough, then there's no point in our continuing this…this…whatever it was. *Flirtation.*"

I stepped around her and rested my hands on her shoulders. "I didn't say I accepted your apology, because there was no reason for you to be sorry. Something came up. You had to leave. I understand. That's it."

"You're acting different."

"I'm not. I'd really like to go to the museum with you. Hell, I'd like to go anywhere with you. Can we please just do that?"

She stared into my eyes long enough that I expected her to turn me down. "Okay." I wished her voice conveyed more enthusiasm, but at least she still wanted to go. I took her hand, and we walked the rest of the way to the farmhouse.

I loved the feel of her hand in mine. Honestly, I just loved the feel of her. The warmth that spread throughout my body was almost enough to make me forget what I'd seen last night. *Almost.*

16

Tara

There were many museums in Florence. So many, in fact, that visiting them became overwhelming and, to some, repetitious.

"God, Tara, not another one," I remembered Penelope complaining when I dragged her, Ava, Aine, and Quinn to *Museo Nazionale di San Marco*. Once inside, though, her attitude had changed, mainly because this wasn't as much a museum as a step back in time.

Rather than galleries, there were thirty small rooms, called cells, in the convent where Fra Angelico and his disciples had painted beautiful frescoes from the New Testament. My favorite was the *Annunciation* fresco on top of the staircase that led to the dormitories. Its intricacies took my breath away.

It depicted the archangel Gabriel visiting the Virgin Mary, but rather than indoors and with Mary enthroned like so many other Gothic paintings of the same theme, in this, they were outdoors.

I looked over at Ben, who instead of looking at the fresco, was studying me.

"Tell me why you love this so much."

I felt my cheeks flush. "Are you bored?"

He cocked his head. "Not even a little." He stepped behind me and put his hands on my shoulders. "I want to see it through your eyes. Tell me why you love it," he repeated.

"Some say the *Annunciation* marked the transition from the Gothic period into the Renaissance. The spatial awareness Fra Angelico achieved is unlike any other iteration. Look at how ethereal they are. And Gabriel's wings." I sighed. "They are so magnificent. I wish I could paint like that."

"Do you? Paint that is?"

I nodded. "You could call it that. I certainly don't have a fraction of Fra Angelico's talent. I dabble."

"What do you like to paint?"

I stepped away from the fresco and walked in the direction of the libraries. "Right now, I'm obsessed with painting Valentini. It seems everywhere I look, the view is more breathtaking than the last." Oddly, this seemed to surprise Ben. "So far I've only done sketches."

"I'd love to see them."

"Why?"

He raised an eyebrow. "Why wouldn't I?"

"They're just sketches."

"So, why not show them to me, then?"

I shook my head. "Too insecure, I suppose."

"I'd bet you are far more talented than you give yourself credit for."

I laughed. "Are you saying that in hopes I'll agree to share a room at the *pensione*?"

He grabbed my hand, jerked me against him, and kissed me. "*That* is me trying to get you to share my *bed* at the *pensione*." He kissed me again. "Feel the difference?"

I licked my lips. "I think so. Maybe you should do it again."

This time his kiss was chaste. "Where to next?"

We wandered the Dominican convent, stopping every so often to admire something I liked or that Ben did. Each time, he stood behind me and rested his hands on my shoulders, telling me again that he wanted to see the work through my eyes. There'd never been anyone, outside of my professors, who were asking for a differ- ent reason, who'd cared about my opinion about much of anything—art in particular.

Thanks to Pia's graciousness in securing our reservation, Ben and I were able to enjoy parts of the convent that weren't always open to the public. Because of this, I'd saved the *Tabernaculum* for last only because I could spend hours studying it. It wasn't just one work of art; it was several.

The rectangular marble frame, with a triangular top with a sculpted almond, depicted the *Blessing of Christ and Cherubims,* and was considered to be a masterpiece in its own right. Some said it housed a different work originally that was eventually replaced by Fra Angelica's paintings.

There were two shutter panels on the front of the *Tabernaculum.* On the external side were paintings of Mark the Evangelist and Saint Peter. Beneath those, on the altarpiece's *predella,* was a triptych of *Saint Peter Dictating the Gospel to Saint Mark, Adoration of the Magi,* and *Martyrdom of Saint Mark.*

The opened panels revealed John the Baptist and John the Evangelist in place of Mark and Peter, flanking the enthroned Virgin Mary and Jesus. Surrounding them were twelve angels, each playing a different musical instrument.

From San Marco, we walked down to the Arno and stood on the iconic Ponte Vecchio, looking at the other bridges and tourists taking photos and shopping for jewelry.

"It is even more breathtaking at dawn," I murmured, remembering how I was the only one of the five of us who came out to admire it.

"I look forward to seeing it," said Ben, turning to me. "Thank you for allowing me to see not just San Marco but Florence through your eyes. I cannot imagine a better view."

Since we'd left Valentini, Ben was back to being flirtatious and sweet, and I was so relieved. I'd spent the last couple of years with people who, more often than not, seemed as though they didn't like me very much. The last thing I wanted was someone else in my life who treated me the same way.

"Do you have a favorite place for dinner in Florence?"

I laughed. "There are far too many to choose from. What about you?"

"I'm afraid my choice would be too *turistico*."

"I'm curious."

Ben smiled. "Maybe I should show you rather than tell you."

We walked for twenty minutes, from the Arno up Borgo Pinti. When Ben led me into the Four Seasons Hotel, I had to concur that some might consider its famed restaurant "touristy." On the other hand, Il Palagio had garnered a Michelin star rating.

"What do you think?" he asked.

"It's lovely." I lowered my voice and leaned closer to him. "It is also *molto costoso*."

"If that is your only concern, I would love to have you join me for dinner."

"I would like that very much. Thank you."

The *maggiordomo* led us to the outside dining area and seated us on the edge of the terrace overlooking the gardens. With our backs to the other diners, it seemed as though we were alone. It was beyond romantic.

Ben rested his arm on the back of my chair and leaned in close to me. "Your smile is beguiling."

It wasn't the first time he'd said it, but I'd never tire of hearing it. The sexiness of his voice made my toes curl. "Thank you," I murmured.

We had a team of servers for our meal along with a sommelier, who not only recommended the perfect pairing for the tasting menu we'd both decided to order but also came to the table with each new wine and shared why he'd chosen it.

I couldn't help but think what a wonderful job that must be. Tasting wine and pairing it with food prepared by a chef like the one at Il Palagio.

From the *amuse-bouche* of red mullet with winter vegetables to the crab timbale with cucumber carpaccio topped with a substantial spoonful of Kaluga Amur caviar, to the chef's signature dish of cavatelli pasta "cacio e pepe" with marinated red prawns and baby squid, everything was sublime.

"You must meet people from around the world," I said when he poured the wine that accompanied our fourth course, Chateaubriand.

"It is one of my favorite things about working for Il Palagio."

By the time we finished our dessert, I was having a hard time keeping my eyes open. I hadn't slept well the night before, after having to abruptly leave the farmhouse and Brand's visit.

"Shall we?" Ben asked when I yawned for the third time.

"Forgive me. I'm more tired than I realized."

He shook his head and stood to help with my chair. "Don't apologize."

I followed him out of the restaurant, baffled when he led me over to the bank of elevators.

"I thought it might be easier if we stayed here tonight."

He withdrew a key card from his pocket. "I've booked a two-bedroom suite."

"Thank you," I murmured, wondering if he expected I'd share his bed or if he truly intended for us to stay in two separate rooms.

Unlike before, when it seemed neither of us could keep our hands off the other, Ben was acting more the polite gentleman.

"I had our bags brought to the room," he said, motioning me to a doorway. When he turned on the light, I saw mine but no others.

He cupped my cheek with his palm and kissed my forehead. "I know you're tired. Get some rest."

I put my hand on the door. "Good night, then."

"Good night, Catarina."

17

Halo

The first thing I did when I entered the second bedroom was put in my earphones. The dual tracking and listening device I'd put in Tara's bag was powerful enough that I'd hear her side of any conversation, unless she put it on speaker, in which case I'd hear both.

So far, she hadn't made any calls, but I expected that once she believed I was out of earshot, there was a good chance she'd contact the man she was supposed to meet.

The time we spent together today had almost made me forget what I'd seen the night before. Tara was engaging, bright, funny, and fascinating. She was also sexy as fuck.

Our day was as close to perfect as I could imagine, if only I could keep seeing her with another man out of my head.

It was hard for me to marry the two sides of her in my mind. How could she be so flirtatious with me if she was involved with someone else? It wasn't just that she flirted, the heat I saw in her eyes sometimes, left me breathless. For hours, I fought against having my hands on her every minute, until I stopped trying and gave in to my desire to touch her.

I heard her moving about, followed by a door closing, which I assumed was the bathroom. I checked my phone to see if there'd been activity on hers, but saw none. When I heard what sounded like Tara filling the bath, I took off my clothes and turned on the shower. Moments later, I heard a faint sound in my ear. Was she crying? I shut off the water and turned the volume up on the earphones.

I rested on the bed and turned off the light, focusing only on the noises I heard coming from the other room. When the sound of the tub filling stopped, I could tell she wasn't crying; Tara was whimpering. More—she was groaning.

My cock sprung to life when I also heard the rustle of water. Evidently, I'd left Miss Emsworth sexually frustrated. I pushed the idea that it wasn't me, but her mystery man, out of my head as I stroked myself in rhythm to her mewls.

She let out a sound similar to the one she made when her eyes rolled back into her head, followed by the one word that brought me to my own quick release. "Ben," she moaned.

I lay still, catching my breath, listening to the water as it moved with what I pictured was her hand between her legs, maybe the fingers of the other pinching her nipples. She said my name again, and I closed my eyes. I saw her on the kitchen island in the farmhouse, writhing against my mouth and fingers. When there was no question she was coming, I stroked myself to my second release.

There was no sound coming from the bathroom or bedroom for quite a while; I'd almost drifted to sleep when I heard her door open and close. I waited, holding my breath to see if she'd come to my room. I could no longer hear her footfalls as I willed the knob of my door to turn. Instead, there was nothing, not even the sound of her walking about.

I pulled on my boxer briefs and went out to the common area. There, by the light of the moon, I could see Tara standing near the window that looked out over the park.

"Is everything okay?" I asked.

She spun around; I'd startled her. "I couldn't sleep," she answered.

After the intimacy she'd unknowingly shared, I had to touch her. I walked over to where she stood and put my arms around her waist. She rested her hands on mine, leaned back into me, and I kissed her neck. Not being able to resist, I moved one hand up to her breast, tucking it inside the hotel's terry-cloth robe, and swirled her nipple with my index finger.

"Catarina," I murmured the name I'd begun thinking of as a term of affection for her.

She turned, put her arms around my neck, reached up, and kissed me. I pushed my tongue between her lips and began the assault on her mouth I'd imagined while I listened as she pleasured herself.

I grabbed her ass with both hands and pulled her against me. It would be so easy for me to lift her in my arms, press my hardness into her heat, and take her in the moonlight, but I couldn't. Not until I knew who the other man was and what he meant to her.

When I released her, she whimpered, but not like before. This was disappointment. I pulled her over to sit beside me on the sofa. "This thing between us… is moving quite fast, Catarina. While I'd like nothing more than to know what it feels like to hold your naked body next to mine, I think we should get to know each other better first, don't you?"

She turned her head away from me and tried to stand, but I wouldn't let her. "Please don't," she whispered when I attempted to get her to look at me.

"If I let you go, it would be the antithesis of our knowing each other better, sweetheart. Talk to me."

When she turned and her eyes met mine, the heat I saw wasn't desire, it was anger. This time when she tried to stand, I let her.

"Get to know each other better? You came in my mouth, Ben, and vice versa. As far as being intimate, I'd say that ranks at the top."

She stumbled when she walked away; I stood to catch her.

"Don't touch me."

I held both her arms. "Why are you angry?"

"Angry? There are several words to describe how I'm feeling, but that isn't one of them. I'm embarrassed, Ben. Humiliated. Please allow me the smallest amount of dignity and let me go."

I released her arms, and she fled into the bedroom, closing rather than slamming the door behind her.

Telling her the truth about why I wasn't ready to have sex with her, not that I could do that, wouldn't have made any difference, except she'd know I was just as humiliated thinking I wasn't the only man in her life.

I stayed awake most of the night, wondering if I'd handled things wrong. I just couldn't imagine looking into her eyes as I sunk deep into her body and not think of what I'd witnessed at the *casina* at Valentini.

When the sun rose, I ordered coffee for her and tea for me. Not long after it arrived, Tara came out of the bedroom.

"Good morning," she murmured without meeting my eyes.

"Good morning, Catarina."

"When did you want to head back?"

I poured her a cup of coffee, added the amount of cream I knew she liked, and brought it to her.

"I could've gotten it, but thank you."

"To answer your question, I thought we'd spend another day in Florence."

Tara looked up at me. "I don't think that is a good idea."

"You might change your mind when I tell you what I have planned for us today."

"Ben, I—"

I put my finger on her lips. "Last night, I told you I want us to get to know each other better. At least hear me out."

She nodded, and I removed my finger.

"I made reservations for us to visit a place I'm sure you've been countless times, but I haven't been once."

I watched as she sipped her coffee, hoping she'd make the mewling sound she did whenever she tasted something she loved. She didn't disappoint me. The downside: it made my cock rock hard.

"Where?"

"The Accademia Gallery."

She smiled. "I've only been once."

"Someone determined to make you as happy as I am suggested the best time to go is later in the afternoon when there are fewer people."

Tara's cheeks flushed. "Sometimes I think Pia is my fairy godmother embodied."

"She cares about you."

"It hasn't been a week since I arrived at Valentini."

I shrugged. Some may find an immediate connection surprising. I didn't. "Kismet."

She walked over to the door that led to a balcony and went outside; I joined her. Looking in one direction, there was a perfect view of the Giardino della Gherardesca. In the other, Brunelleschi's Dome. Something occurred to me.

"Do you carry a sketchbook with you?"

"I don't, but I should." She waved her arm. "Isn't it magnificent?"

"Do you think it's too late to catch the views from Ponte Vecchio?"

"Not if we leave now." Tara took another sip of her coffee and set it down on the tray. "Ready?"

After watching the sunrise from Florence's most famous bridge, we had breakfast at an outdoor café with views of the Arno and then walked the side streets of the city.

"Look," I said, pointing across the cobbled road at a shop that looked as though it sold art supplies. "Do you want to go in?"

"You wouldn't mind?"

"I don't mind anything that brings a smile to your face."

It was obvious to me that while Tara had been brought up in what most would consider a charmed life, having someone pay attention to the things she liked or was interested in, surprised her.

While she took her time perusing the paints, brushes, and canvases, I pretended to be doing the same. Instead, I watched her. "Nothing?" I asked when I saw her walk toward the shop's door.

She shrugged. "I don't know that I'll have time to paint."

"What if I commissioned you?"

Tara laughed out loud. "To do what?"

"Paint Valentini."

"You're being ridiculous."

"I'm not. In fact, maybe I'll be inspired to write a story about it."

"I suppose I could paint when I'm not working in the tasting room, not that I'm taking your joke about a commission seriously. I'm just rethinking the time I might have."

We left the shop several minutes later, my arms laden with all sorts of painting supplies. While she was gathering them, I sneaked a purchase of a leather-bound sketchbook that I dropped into one of her bags when she wasn't looking.

We took the bags to the hotel and then found a place near the Accademia Gallery, where we could have an espresso while we waited for our reservation time. We'd been seated a few minutes when Tara pulled out the book I'd intended to be a surprise along with a pencil.

"Thank you for this," she said, opening it to the first page.

I watched in fascination as she drew the front facade of the museum, complete with the tourists without reservations waiting in the standby line.

She turned her chair and turned the page, sketching another view from where we sat. Soon, she had five pages filled.

"May I see?"

"They're just sketches," she said but handed me the book anyway.

"What is this?" I asked, pointing to something I'd noticed she put at the top of each page. It looked like a gradient.

"It's the balance of light to dark values."

I nodded as though I understood what that meant and studied her drawings. "These alone are good, I can't imagine how it will look when you paint it."

"I'm not that good, Ben. You might want to lower your expectations."

She took the book from my hands and filled several more pages. I almost didn't want to tell her it was time for us to go into the museum.

18

Tara

I put the sketchbook back in my bag and stood to follow Ben to the entrance of the Accademia. I'd walked a few steps when the hair on the back of my neck stood up. I looked across the street, expecting to see Brand. I didn't, but the person I saw instead was definitely watching me. Even when my eyes met his, he didn't look away. Nor did he smile.

Like Ben, the man was very muscular, so much so that his clothes strained against his bulk. I reached for Ben's arm and tucked mine through it.

Instead of looking at me, he looked across the cobbled road, perhaps sensing someone watching us like I had. He put his hand on my waist and moved me so I was walking on the other side of him, farther from the man whose gaze still had not wavered. Not only that, he began walking too, in the same direction we were.

Ben ducked me into the next shop door we came to. I peeked around him and saw that the man kept walking. He moved me to his side, and I watched him rest his hand on something.

"Is that a gun?" I whispered.

"Shh." He looked over his shoulder, and I did the same. No one appeared to be paying any attention to us.

After a couple of minutes, we went back out and continued our walk toward the museum, only this time, he had me tucked against his side.

"Why do you have a gun?" I asked.

His eyes scanned our surroundings. "I told you the work I do is investigative."

Not long after I'd been kidnapped, I thought about getting a permit to carry a gun, but had never followed through with it. Right now, I wished I had.

Yesterday, when we entered the Museo di San Marco, I hadn't been paying attention to Ben when he stopped and talked with one of the security guards. Today I did.

"What did you show him?" I asked when he walked over to where I stood waiting.

"My carry permit."

He led me over to the elevator and down to the first floor where the Giovanni da Milano and the late four-teenth century rooms were located. It wasn't a place most visitors of the museum ever went. The focus here was on the techniques employed by artists like da Milano, Michelangelo, and Cennino.

We spent almost three hours in the Accademia, both of us—or at least me—trying to forget about the man we saw before we came in. There was something so sinister about him that I couldn't shake the feeling that overcame me when my eyes met his.

While Ben had said the work he did was investigative, it wasn't an explanation nor did it assuage my fear.

"How much of an inconvenience would it be if we returned to Valentini tonight?" I asked when we were nearing the museum's exit. "I'd be more than willing to cover the cost of the room."

Ben stopped walking and led me away from the walkway. "Of course we can return to Valentini if you'd be more comfortable, and no, you cannot cover the cost of the hotel room."

"But—"

He grasped the back of my neck and brought his face close to mine. "We're going to talk when we get back to Val d'Orcia, but know this, I don't intend for you to spend another night in your *casina* alone."

"What are you talking about?"

"You'll stay with me in the farmhouse."

With scrunched eyes, I studied him. "Who are you?"

What he said next was the last thing I expected. "Maybe I'll answer that when you tell me who you are."

Neither of us spoke during the two-hour drive back to Valentini. After a while, I rested my head against the seat and closed my eyes, trying not to let my paranoia over what Ben had said spin out of control.

Did he know who I really was? There was so much about him that reminded me not just of Ava's husband, Razor, but of all the men he worked with. Was that who Ben really was? Was he here in Tuscany to find me? Or, like Razor had with Ava, was he here to protect me?

No. That couldn't be. What reason would anyone have to protect me? Which meant if his cryptic comment implied what I feared it did, he was either here to find me or use me to find my father.

I couldn't stay in the farmhouse with him, though; I had to talk to Brand. After Ben had insinuated himself into my plans to visit Florence, I'd sent him a message explaining why I'd be unable to meet him. Although, my plan hadn't been to do as he asked. I'm sure he assumed I'd be traveling back to New York as he demanded; however, I wasn't going anywhere until I found my father.

Maybe it would be better if I left Val d'Orcia and traveled to a different part of Italy. It was only that Vi believed my father would be in Tuscany that led me here.

When we pulled through the gates of Valentini, Ben drove straight up to the *casina*. When he cut the car's engine, I got out and waited near the back of it.

"Let's get your things," he said, motioning to the front door.

"I'm not staying with you."

"The man you saw, the one that scared the shit out of you, wasn't after me, sweetheart."

"What makes you think he was after either of us?"

He raised a brow. "Do you really want to have this conversation now? Here?"

"Why not?"

"You know the answer to that." Ben walked over, put his hand on the doorknob, and it fell open. He took two steps backwards and drew his gun.

"Get back in the car," he said in a hushed tone.

"Was someone in there?" I asked as he drove down to the farmhouse.

"I don't know, but I'm not going to risk it."

Ben drove down, parked in front of the farmhouse, turned off the car, but didn't get out. He pulled his cell out of his pocket. I heard a man's voice with an Italian accent answer.

"Who else do you have at Valentini?" Ben asked. I couldn't hear the man's response.

"At least two, as soon as possible."

"What are we doing?" I asked when he dropped the phone into his lap.

"Waiting."

"For?"

"Backup."

19

Halo

While I didn't get a good look into the *casina*, I saw enough to know that someone had been in there. My guess was, they were looking more for Richard Emsworth than for his daughter, but I couldn't be certain of that.

If I found out that Lucia or anyone else from AISE had been in there, I'd have her removed not just from Valentini but from her job.

Later, once I was sure there was adequate detail for Tara, I'd call a meeting and conference in Striker. If necessary, I'd bring Doc in too.

I turned toward Tara. "My name is Benjamin Knox Clarkson. My friends and the people I work with call me Halo."

"Who do you work for?"

"K19 Security Solutions."

She nodded in understanding.

"You should be aware that I am in Italy on behalf of the CIA."

"Because of my father?"

I nodded. "Initially, my only concern was finding you. Once we discovered your father had disappeared too, we specifically asked for the assignment."

"Who did?"

"Quinn's father, Doc."

Tara put her head in her hands. When I saw her shoulders heave, I longed to reach over and comfort her, but there was more we needed to talk about before I could allow myself to do that.

"Catarina," I murmured, putting my hand on her arm.

She turned to me. "You don't have to call me that. You know my name."

"I like it."

She covered her tear-stained face with her hands a second time.

"What's making you cry?"

When Tara shook her head, I moved her hand from her face, put her arm around my waist, and pulled her into my arms. Seeing her like this, I couldn't remember what I thought we needed to talk about first.

My phone vibrated with a text message, but I ignored it. "Can you tell me why you're crying?"

"Why did they want to find me?"

"I don't understand the question."

"Why did *Doc* want to find me?"

"Because he cares about you. Everyone does."

I could feel her head shake against my shoulder and pulled back enough that I could look into her eyes. "Tara, *everyone* cares about you."

"They think I stole from them," she whispered.

"Who does?"

"Pen, Aine, Ava. Maybe even Quinn."

"I haven't heard anything about that. When I talked to each of them, their only concern was finding you. At any cost, by the way."

"What do you mean?"

"Your four best friends offered to pay for K19 to find you. Regardless of the cost."

She looked at me as though she was trying to gauge whether I was telling her the truth.

"They love you, Tara."

Evidently, that hadn't been the right thing to say since it made her cry harder. When my phone vibrated again, I sneaked a glance at it. There was a text from Lucia, saying the farmhouse was cleared for entry and that two people from AISE were assigned to it. Another team had cleared the *casina* and were collecting evidence.

"Let's go inside," I said, moving Tara so I could get out of the car.

I sent a text to Lucia, asking her to have Tara's belongings moved down here and that I'd explain what was happening to Pia. I also sent a text to Mateo, requesting a meeting tomorrow.

Since we'd left the museum and immediately went from the hotel to where I'd had to leave my car, we hadn't had time for dinner. My guess was Tara would say she wasn't hungry, but I had to eat. Fortunately, I had plenty of food left.

"Have a seat," I said, motioning to the sofa. "I'm going to have a glass of wine. Would you like to join me?"

"Yes, please."

I was disappointed when Tara didn't follow me into the kitchen, but I had just told her to take a seat. I came back moments later, handed her a glass, and sat beside her. "You and I have a lot to talk about."

She set her glass down and folded her hands in front of her. I pulled them apart.

"We're talking. You're not in trouble."

She wiggled out of my grasp. "You're going to ask about my father."

Not just her father, but the man I'd seen her with too, although that part could wait.

"How long have you been following me?" she asked.

I took a sip of wine, realizing it hadn't elicited a moan out of her when it almost did me.

"When I walked into the tasting room and saw you, I thought my eyes were playing tricks on me. Since then."

She took another drink of wine and looked off into the distance.

"What else do you want to ask me?" I asked.

"Nothing I want the answer to."

"Come here." I pulled her into my arms. "I changed my mind. We don't need to talk tonight." I felt her body relax and then stiffen again when there was a knock at the door.

"That's someone bringing your things from the *casina*." When she moved away and went to stand, I put my hand on her arm. "I'll get it."

I opened the door and saw Lucia standing on the other side. She looked beyond me at Tara. "Can I come in?"

I didn't like it, but I let her.

"Tara, this is Agent Lucia Cesare. She is with AISE, Italy's intelligence agency."

"Agent Cesare, I believe you know Tara Emsworth."

Tara visibly bristled.

"I'm sorry if I came off rude to you. That wasn't my intention," said Lucia.

"Thank you," Tara responded.

I stepped forward and took Tara's bag from Lucia. "I'll just take this upstairs…later," I added when Tara's eyes opened wide.

"I'll be going, then. *Arrivederci.*"

Relieved the agent wasn't trying to push Tara to talk, I closed the door behind Lucia and sat on the sofa where I'd been before we heard the knock. "Where were we?" I asked, pulling her back into my arms, happy when she came willingly. "By the way, she's here at Valentini for another reason. Something that has nothing to do with you." It occurred to me that I shouldn't have said that. "Something Pia knows nothing about, but it is to her benefit."

"In other words, you don't want me to say anything to her."

I angled my face so I could see hers. She didn't appear angry.

"I know I said we didn't need to talk tonight, but I would like to talk about you and me."

"The last thing I want to talk about," she muttered.

"Ouch." I tightened my grip. "Maybe, instead, I'll tell you a story." I saw a slight smile on her face. "The same day you 'disappeared,' I almost died in a plane crash."

"You did?"

"Yep. I was on a mission, heading to Columbia, and the plane I was on took a dive. As you can see, I lived through it."

"Did everyone?"

I shook my head but had no intention of telling her why not. "My best friend was on the same plane, and he lived too. We call him Tackle. Anyway, there's a point I'm trying to make. I called him the other day, the morning after you, Pia, and I first spent the afternoon and evening together. I told him about you."

She angled her head and buried it in my shoulder. "Are you going to tell me what you said?"

"I am."

"Do you have to?"

"You're assuming it was something bad."

She shrugged like she had earlier.

"I told him that you and I connected. Straight off. I asked him what he thought I should do."

"Did he tell you to run as fast and as far as you could?"

There'd be time for me to figure out why Tara had such a low opinion of herself, but now, I needed to reassure her.

"He said I should reach out and grab every bit of happiness I could. When I asked if that would be the case even if it affected my job, he told me to fuck my job."

"That doesn't sound like very good advice."

"Maybe not to someone who hasn't been in a plane crash."

"Ben…um…is that what I should call you?"

I thought about the first night she was at the farmhouse and how when I came inside her the first time, I wanted to be able to call out her name. Her real name. I also wanted to hear my real name on her lips.

"Call me Knox."

"Knox…"

"Yes?"

"I forgot what I was going to ask you. I like that name better than Ben, by the way. No offense."

"Ben is my dad. And no offense taken."

"What does your story mean?"

"That this is real." I tilted her head with my fingers, so my lips could reach hers and kissed her. Relief spread throughout my body when she wrapped her arms around my neck and kissed me back. "You know, kissing you reminds me of the dinner we started the other night and never finished, which also reminds me that I'm starving."

"I'm hungry too."

I almost asked if it was for food, but there was more Tara and I had to talk about before I started dropping sexual innuendos.

Being in the kitchen with her, preparing much the same food as I'd started the last time, proved to be an exercise in restraint I was certain I'd fail. Noticing the flush on her cheeks, I could guess Tara was remembering the same things I was.

"Excuse me," she murmured and left the kitchen. I could hear her footfalls first on the stairs and then in the bedroom above where I stood, the same one she'd slept in before, and where I'd put her belongings.

A few minutes later, she was back, sketchbook in hand. I looked out the windows at the night sky, wondering what she planned to draw. A few seconds later, she plopped down in a chair, facing me.

"Please tell me you're sketching the refrigerator."

She laughed but didn't put down her pencil.

I tried to catch a peek every so often while I cooked, but her arm was in the way. "Are you going to show me?"

"Maybe."

By the time I finished preparing our dinner, Tara had filled several pages with sketches. I walked over to the table and held the plates while she put the book away.

"Wait," I said, setting my dinner down. "Show me what you drew tonight."

She looked up at me and raised a brow. "Are you seriously going to hold my food hostage until I show you?"

"Yep."

"I'll warn you that I'm going to go back and add horns to every sketch of you."

I shrugged. "Let me see."

"If that didn't smell so good and I wasn't starving, you'd never get away with this."

When Tara opened the book and showed me a couple of the pages, I was stunned, particularly since I'd watched how quickly she drew each image. I set her plate in front of her. "You can have my dinner too. That's how good those are."

"You're just saying that because I made you look so handsome."

I studied the image and looked up at her. "Nah, I am that handsome. Look how much more attractive you made the refrigerator look, though."

She smiled, something I wouldn't have predicted she'd do earlier. I couldn't stop myself. I stood from the seat I'd just taken and kissed her. I wanted her, every bit of her, but I couldn't have her. Not yet. Not until we talked about the guy I'd seen in the *casina*.

"What?" she asked when I sat back down.

"What, what?"

"You were joking around, and now you're…it's like you're angry."

"I'm not angry."

She set her fork down and folded her arms.

"We'll talk about it later."

"The thing you're not angry about?"

"Tara…just eat."

Did she? Of course she didn't. She got up and began cleaning up the kitchen. I shoved a couple more forkfuls of food into my mouth, just because I *was* that hungry, and then stood.

"Come here." I pulled her out the door that went from the kitchen to the *terrazza*. Once we were outside, I tugged her onto my lap. This wasn't going to be an easy conversation for either of us. I needed her close to me just as much as I guessed she'd need the same thing.

"The night you left, before we could have dinner, I followed you."

She tried to get up, but I tightened my grip.

"I saw you with a man." I rested my head against hers. "When I saw the two of you embrace, I hated it."

Tara turned her head and angled it away from me. "It wasn't like that."

"Like what?"

"I was happy to see him—"

"You were ecstatic to see him."

She tried to get off my lap a second time.

"No, Tara. Keep talking."

"It wasn't romantic, Ben."

"Knox."

"Whatever."

"No. Not whatever. Say my name."

"It wasn't romantic, *Knox*."

"Does he know that?"

"Definitely."

I kissed the side of her neck. "I can't tell you how happy that makes me."

"Aren't you going to ask—"

"No. Not tonight. Tonight is about you and me. No one else."

"Ben?"

"Knox."

"Oh my God. *Knox*. Last night. Was it because you thought…"

"The truth?" I took a deep breath. "Yes."

"It wasn't because you didn't…want me?"

"I heard you when you were in the bath, Tara. I couldn't understand how it was possible for you to call out my name, pleasure yourself that way, with *my* name on your lips, if there was someone else."

Her cheeks turned bright red when she realized what I was talking about. "You didn't answer my question."

"No, it wasn't because I didn't want you. I can't keep my hands off you. I'm surprised you haven't noticed."

"I noticed."

I gripped her face with my hand and looked into her eyes. "I want you, Tara."

"I want you too, *Knox*."

She smirked and I kissed her. When she opened her mouth to me, I angled my head, going deeper. Tara shifted so she was straddling me and wrapped her arms around my neck.

"Should we go back inside?" she asked.

"Sure." Before she could get off my lap, I stood and carried her over to the door. She reached out and opened it. I walked through and kicked it closed behind me. I set her in her chair before going into the kitchen to get her plate.

"I guess you want to eat."

"We *need* to eat, Tara."

"We do?"

My mouth was full, so I nodded and pointed at her plate. "You're going to need your strength," I said after I swallowed.

"I am?"

"Oh, yeah."

20

Tara

I stabbed a mushroom with my fork and put it in my mouth. How could I not think about the last time we were in this kitchen, eating food Knox prepared for me.

Looking over at him, it was obvious he was thinking about the same thing I was. How easy it would be to get lost in sex and avoid thinking about everything that had happened today. Could I do that? Bury my head and pretend my life was as simple as it looked on the surface?

Knox was aware it wasn't. He knew I was in Italy because my father had disappeared. What he knew beyond that, we hadn't talked about.

Did he suspect why I'd come to Italy specifically? Did he know about the millions of dollars sitting in an account in a Zürich bank under my assumed identity?

One question I didn't have to ask was what he knew about Brand. When he told me he'd seen us, it was obvious he didn't even know his name.

It was imperative I find time to get in touch with him to let him know that not only had I been discovered, I had no intention of leaving Italy.

Or maybe I should just come clean now and let Knox help me. He would, wouldn't he?

He reached over and grasped my hand. "You have a lot on your mind."

"I do."

"I told you we didn't have to talk about it tonight. However, if you want to, we certainly can."

I took a deep breath and let it out slowly. Was I really considering trusting this man I barely knew? It wasn't just my life that would be impacted if I did. My father's would be too.

"We've had a long day. Why don't you sleep on it and decide tomorrow how comfortable you feel confiding in me?"

I studied him and shook my head.

"What?" he asked.

"Is it really that simple, Ben…err…Knox? I can decide how comfortable I am?"

"For now, yes. It really is that simple."

"When does it become more complicated?"

He sat back in his chair. "Two things concern me above the rest. First, the man we saw earlier today in Florence. Second, that someone was in the *casina*. Apart from that, there's nothing I see as urgent, unless you know who he is and why he was following you. Or if there are additional threats against your safety you're aware of."

"I don't know any of those things."

He stood and took his plate to the sink but looked as though he had something more to say. Like I had, he took a deep breath and let it out slowly. "Tara, the man I saw you with, do you have any reason to believe he would do anything to hurt you?"

"None whatsoever. I know he would never."

"That's good enough for me."

"For now?"

He smiled. "For now."

After we cleaned up the dishes from dinner, Knox took my hand and led me over to the staircase. "I want you to sleep in my bed tonight, Tara."

"Okay."

"There's something you need to understand first."

"I don't like the sound of that."

"Which is why we're talking about it before we go upstairs."

I nodded even though I really didn't want to hear what he was about to say.

"I want you in bed beside me. I want to feel you next to me. And as much as I want to have sex with you, we aren't going to. Not tonight."

There was no need for me to look in the mirror to confirm my cheeks were flushed. I could feel the heat in them. The humiliation I felt made me want to race out of the farmhouse. Knox, obviously anticipating that reaction, had his arm around my waist and was holding on tightly.

"Too much happened today. I know you're feeling that as much as I am. I'm not saying it won't happen tomorrow, but even if it doesn't, it won't change the fact that I want you."

He cupped my flaming cheek with his palm. "I know that, somewhere inside, you agree this is the best thing for both of us." His eyes bored into mine. "Don't you, Tara?"

I had to admit, I did. My first reaction was embarrassment, but if I'd allowed myself time to think it through, I knew what he was saying was best for both of us.

"One more thing—"

Before he could speak, I put my fingers on his lips.

"Let me say it."

I rolled my eyes.

"I told you I want you in bed beside me. If you don't want that, I'm not going to force you, Tara."

"I would really like to sleep with you, Knox."

He smiled and led me up the staircase, past the room where my things were.

"Sorry, I'm kind of a slob," he muttered, picking up the clothes scattered around the room and tossing them into a heap in the corner.

I went back into the hallway and to the room where my bags were. I grabbed a few things and used the restroom. When I came back into the bedroom, Knox was sitting at the end of the bed. He was wearing fleece shorts but no shirt. And, God, he looked delicious. I'd never been with a man like him before—someone so muscular. His upper arms were bigger around than my thighs. The idea of all that power thrusting into me made me shudder.

He held out his hand, and I came and sat beside him.

"You sure you're okay with this?" he asked.

"I don't think I'd sleep otherwise."

He smiled.

"You like being the protector, don't you?"

His cheeks flushed, which made me want to pinch them as much as kiss him.

"I guess I kind of do."

I got up and walked around him so I was on the side of the bed farther from the door. Knox smiled again before turning off the lights and climbing in beside me. He held out his arm, and I shifted closer to him and rested my head on his bare chest.

"I like having you in my arms." When he bent down and kissed me, I could taste the toothpaste he'd just used like I had. "I want to know everything about you, Tara." He kissed my forehead. "That wasn't supposed to make you tense," he added a few seconds later.

"I hope you like what you find."

Knox turned on his side so he was facing me. "You are bright and beautiful and talented and smart. I've learned so much from you in the last few days. You fascinate me. The only thing I don't understand is why you don't believe all of those things about yourself. In fact, I think once you get to know me better, you may discover you are way out of my league."

I leaned forward and kissed him. "I doubt that." I closed my eyes, not surprised by how tired I was, but by how quickly I felt myself falling to sleep.

"Thank you, Knox," I murmured.

"You're welcome, Tara."

When I woke the next morning, Knox was still asleep. I reached out and ran my fingers over the definition in his abs. What did it take to maintain a physique like his? He must spend hours every day in the gym. Although, where would he work out here?

I giggled when Knox grabbed my fingers with his hand and brought them to his lips. He pulled me so the top half of my body rested on the top half of his.

"I kept waking up, making sure you were still beside me."

"Did you really think I'd leave?" I asked.

"There's a good chance I snore."

I smiled and nodded. "You do."

The phone on the table beside the bed vibrated; he reached over and picked it up.

"Sorry. I need to take this."

I got up to use the restroom. Knox had a loud voice, so the fact that I couldn't hear him, meant he was intentionally speaking quietly. I eased out of the bathroom door, went downstairs, and filled a teapot with water. While it heated, I looked around for coffee, relieved when I found a French press and some espresso already ground.

"Where did you run off to?" I heard Knox say from the stairwell.

"Making you a cup of tea."

He didn't say anything else, and I didn't hear him come down the stairs. A few minutes later, he did. He came up behind me and put his arms around my waist. "I was really hoping I wasn't dreaming." He kissed my cheek while I dunked the tea bag into the hot water in his cup.

"Am I doing it right?"

He laughed. "Hard to do it wrong. How would you feel about going up to the villa for breakfast?"

"You did tell Lucia that you would talk to Pia."

"That was Lucia who called actually. Pia is none the wiser about what went down at the *casina.*"

"Oh. Then, we could stay here."

"We need to talk about you working in Valentini's tasting room."

"Oh," I repeated.

"I have someone from K19 looking for security footage from yesterday to see if we can identify the man on the street, but I'm not sure how long that might take. Even if we do, that doesn't mean we can protect you in a place as public as the tasting room."

"I understand," I said, turning my back to hide the disappointment I felt. I knew it was silly, but I'd felt such a sense of pride whenever someone bought even a bottle of wine after tasting with me. When they bought a case, it was even more rewarding.

"I have an idea."

I turned back to face Knox. "What?"

"Why don't you spend the time you'd be working in the winery, painting Valentini instead? Maybe Pia would sell your artwork."

"I truly appreciate your confidence in me, Knox, but you haven't seen any of my work other than sketches."

"All I'm saying is to give it a shot."

"What am I going to tell Pia about why I have to quit?"

"I'm not sure yet."

"I was afraid you were going to say that. Everything I've come up with makes me sound like a spoiled brat."

Had I really said that out loud? It was definitely how I saw myself, but since when had I become so effusive about sharing my innermost thoughts?

"Like everything else I said to you last night about how fabulously amazing you are, I have trouble with that assessment. I would use neither spoiled nor brat when describing you."

"You're more generous with me than others."

"I'm going to make it my goal to help you see you are so much more than you believe yourself to be."

My eyes met Knox's when we heard a knock at the door. "I hope that isn't Pia," I whispered.

21

Halo

It was Pia, and based on the look on her face, Lucia's assessment of her being oblivious to what had happened in Tara's *casina* was far off base.

She looked over my shoulder and raced past me.

"Can you forgive me?" she said to a wide-eyed Tara.

"What for?"

"That someone broke into your *casina*." Pia shook her head and looked down at the floor. "I do not understand the things that are happening at Valentini. I am not cut out for this."

The last sentence, she murmured in defeat. Like Tara, Pia was criticizing herself for things she shouldn't be. It was Tara, even myself, who'd incited the break-in, albeit as much unknowingly as unintentionally.

My eyes met Tara's, and I pointed at my chest. She nodded.

"Pia, the last thing I want to do is make you feel worse for something beyond your control, but given that it appeared Catarina may have been targeted specifically, I'm going to suggest she take a few days off from the tasting room. The decision is, of course, up to the two of you."

"I understand." Pia dropped Tara's hand.

The look on the two women's faces crushed me.

"I'm probably overreacting. You know how I get about our Catarina," I said with a smile.

"How do you feel?" Pia asked Tara.

"I'd be very sad if I couldn't be in the tasting room." She turned to me, mouthing, "Thank you."

"How much of a disruption would I be if I spent time there writing?"

Pia's smile was broad. "You are *incantato* with my friend, *sì?*"

I wasn't certain of the word's translation, but if it meant infatuated with, crazy about, then, yes. I was. I had a feeling the next words to come out of my mouth might get me in a little trouble, but it was worth it. "Pia, were you aware Catarina is an artist?"

As anticipated, Tara glared at me.

"You are?" Pia asked, taking Tara's hand in hers again. "What is your medium?"

"Painting. Oils and watercolor mainly, depending on the subject matter."

I could see Pia's face; she was just as in awe of Tara as I was.

"You amaze me," she said. "You are a woman of the Renaissance."

"I suggested she paint some of the Valentini landscapes that you might be able to sell at the winery."

"That idea is *fantastica*. Do you have any I could see?"

"Knox's—I mean Ben's—suggestion is premature. I've only done a few sketches so far." I winked when Tara looked at me with scrunched eyes.

"It relieves me that you are staying at the farmhouse with Ben as much as it saddens me that Valentini has not been a safe place for you." Pia took a deep breath. "I will see you later, *sì*?"

"We were thinking of coming up to the villa for breakfast."

"I would love that," she said, breaking into one of her signature smiles.

"You are in trouble," Tara scolded when Pia left.

I nodded. "I'm happy to take any punishment you want to mete out."

"Even if it is that I refuse to paint?"

She had me there. "Except that."

After breakfast, Tara and I went to the tasting room, where I settled with my laptop at a table tucked off to the side of the room. I had many emails to sort through but filtered those from K19 from the rest.

Doc reported that there was still no word on who the man I saw in Tara's *casina* was. However, not surprisingly, there was an immediate hit on the man we'd seen in Florence.

Liborio Strollo was a mid-level enforcer for the 'Ndrangheta syndicate. *"Il mento,"* as he was known, meant "the chin."

If Tara's father did, in fact, have ties to the organization, it would be hard to predict his reasons for following her. Was he looking for Richard Emsworth like we were? Or was he looking for Tara on behalf of her father? Not knowing exactly what her father's connections were, made it impossible to guess.

The next email I read, cleared some of that up for me. It also sent chills up my spine. According to Razor, the wire fraud charges against Emsworth were for art forgery as well as art fraud. As Money had said, to the tune of millions of dollars.

He was accused of selling forgeries of lesser-known masters throughout Europe, but in Italy primarily. Some of the same painters whose works Tara and I had seen at the two museums in Florence were mentioned on the list of forgeries.

In addition, Emsworth was accused of selling multiple shares of works that were higher in value. In one instance, it was said he sold more than forty ten-percent shares of the same painting. Each share sold was reported to be for a million dollars.

Tara hadn't mentioned her father was an artist. Something made me doubt he was. So who had produced the forgeries he'd peddled all over the continent?

I reviewed the attachments Razor had sent on the indictments. Interestingly, no victims from the States had come forward. There was also no mention of a co-conspirator. However, the charge of enterprise corruption would indicate there should have been.

When there was a lull in tasting-room traffic, Tara came over to the table. "Am I interrupting?"

"Not at all," I said, standing to pull out the chair next to me. "How's your day been so far?"

Her smile was broad, and her eyes sparkled. "We're selling a lot of wine. Good, since that's the goal."

"I've become obsessed with the idea of you painting. I'm beginning to feel like a pest."

"Rightly so."

I smiled. "Is anyone else in your family as artistic as you are?"

Her eyes hooded. "No. Why do you ask?"

I didn't like her response any more than she liked my question. I'd hit on something; I was certain of it. "Just part of me learning everything I can about you."

"Better get back to work." She stood and walked away.

Fuck. Why did my every instinct scream she was hiding something?

That night and the next morning, Tara had pulled back from me, reinforcing my suspicions. I'd also happened upon her typing something into her phone, stayed hidden, and watched while she continued an exchange.

I let her off the hook that first night, saying too much had taken place that day and we could put off talking about why she was in Italy. The time had come for us to have the conversation I knew in my gut would drive us even farther apart.

Before we did that, I needed to schedule a meeting with Mateo Casavetti. Something else I'd been putting off. In order to do that, my preference was that Tara stay at the farmhouse. Given she'd worked the last two days and the tasting room was closed tomorrow, I contacted the AISE agent, asking him to confirm we could meet the following day and that he could provide additional backup here at Valentini.

"I have a meeting in Florence tomorrow," I said to Tara later, as we sat on the *terrazza,* having dinner prepared for us by Nonna Bella. Pia had begged off, saying she had work to do, but my guess was it was really to allow Tara and I to have a romantic evening.

She nodded and put another forkful of food into her mouth.

"While I'm gone, I'd like you to remain at the farmhouse. There will be people there making sure you're safe." She didn't react in any way. "Tara?"

She looked over her shoulder to see if anyone had heard my gaffe. "Um, yes, thank you, Ben."

"Please look at me."

She set down her fork and did as I asked.

"While you may not realize it, I'm on your side. You can trust me, Catarina."

"Can I?"

I'd been giving her space, waiting for her to open back up to me. Maybe that was the wrong approach. I reached over and took her hand. "You can trust me," I repeated.

"You say that, but…"

I shook my head. "I say that because I mean it."

She shook her head too. "You hardly know me," she whispered. It was a recurring theme, one I had little argument against. How could I say in one breath that I did know her while, in the other, say how I wanted to learn everything about her? They were contradictory statements. Was there something I could say instead? I thought back to my childhood and the words my parents repeated to my sister and me often.

"No matter what you get yourself involved in, whether you're in trouble or in over your head in some other way, you can come to your mother and me. We'll always help." I said the words to Tara in the way my father said them to me. "I grew up knowing I never had to overcome anything I believed was insurmountable on my own." I lowered my voice. "I'm making the same promise to you, Tara. No matter what it is, or even who it is, I will help you."

"That's a promise?"

I crossed my heart and raised my hand like some kind of damn nine-year-old Boy Scout. "It's a promise."

Tara nodded. She wasn't ready to talk, but she had listened. For now, that was as much as I could ask for.

When I left the next morning to drive to Florence, I was filled with anxiety. I didn't track of the number of missions I'd been involved in over the course of my career, but there was one thing I knew to be true of every one of them. I hadn't been anxiety-ridden. There were many times I'd acknowledged going in, that I may not live through it. There'd been times, like the plane crash, when I knew I wouldn't. Anxiety, though, was not a feeling I was accustomed to.

I thought about calling Tackle, but felt like too much of a pussy to go through with it. Besides, to my knowledge, he'd never been on a mission where the asset, target, whomever, was someone he was personally involved with.

Several of the other K19 guys had been, including all four of the founding partners. No way in hell I'd talk to any of them about it.

While Tara and I still hadn't had sex, last night, she'd clung to me, both awake and asleep. I didn't press, trusting that when she was ready, she'd talk to me.

Before I left, I gave her a kiss so hard that I tasted the metallic tang of blood. "I'm sorry," I murmured, but Tara pulled me back in for more.

Finally, knowing that if I didn't leave then, I wouldn't leave at all, I'd pulled her arms from around my neck and taken a step back. "I'll be gone four hours, tops. You're safe here, Tara. I wouldn't leave if I doubted that for a minute."

The look in her eyes haunted me still. She was truly afraid, and I hated leaving her feeling that way. I knew, though, that once I did and came back, each time I had to leave after this, would be easier for her.

22

Tara

I wasn't certain what Knox knew about my past. Probably more than I'd want him to. But how much did he know about the kidnapping? I shuddered like I did every time I thought about it. I'd never been so afraid in my life. I didn't doubt he'd faced worse. I mean, he told me he'd almost died in a plane crash, for God's sake.

He'd said that facing certain death made him want to reach out and grab every happiness he could.

My ordeal didn't have the same effect on me. Instead of reaching out to grab anything, I turned inward. I almost never went anywhere alone. It was sheer adrenaline that got me from the States here alone, and then kept me going until I arrived at Valentini. I suppose knowing I had no choice was really what drove me.

I grabbed my burner phone and went out to the *terrazza*, wondering if I'd be heard more outside or less. Would Knox or someone else have bugged the farmhouse? Were the people "protecting" me also listening to every word I said?

It didn't surprise me Brand's phone played a message that the number was invalid. He must've gotten a new burner phone after I sent him the text messages saying my identity had been discovered and I would not leave Italy.

I went upstairs, grabbed the bags of art supplies I'd purchased, and brought them downstairs to organize.

After dividing everything into two sets—one for watercolor and one for when I painted oils—I put the latter back into the bags. Today, I'd start with watercolor since it would be far less complicated to clean up.

I pulled out my sketchbook and thumbed through the pages, trying to decide what to paint first. Finally, after changing my mind several times, I decided on the view of the Giardino della Gherardesca I'd drawn from the balcony of the hotel. While my sketch was in black and white, I could recall the variances between the deep and lighter green hues so vividly. Not a lot of other color had popped out at me, given the time of year, but one sculpture had.

It was a dark bronze of a naked woman. The shape of her body was so much like my own, with small breasts and a slight frame, unlike most of the sculpture I'd seen of women in this part of Italy. I flipped the page until I came to it and then set about marrying the images together. While I'd normally start with a smaller study, with this painting, I went straight to a quarter-sheet.

The trick with watercolor was to never overwork the image. With oils, I could paint over anything I didn't think looked just right. With the water-based medium, once I overcorrected, I could paint on the other side of the sheet once it dried, or dump the whole thing in the garbage.

Since I was embellishing anyway, I took the liberty of changing the hair on the sculpture. It was shoulder-length, but I extended it to her waist—more like mine.

I forced myself to step away and went out to the *terrazza* to enjoy the afternoon sun. I hadn't seen a soul, but had no doubt they were nearby.

"There she is," I heard Knox say. I opened and then shielded my eyes from the sun.

"You're back."

"I am. You've been busy. I'll confess to peeking."

"You could hardly do otherwise since I left it on the easel."

He sat in the chair beside me and rested his forearms on the table. "It's really beautiful, Tara."

The reverence I heard in his voice filled me with more pride than if I'd sold several cases of Valentini wine. "Thank you. It's a gift for you, Knox."

He sat back and put his hand on his heart. "I didn't dare hope." There was no playfulness in his voice, no sarcasm, just sincerity. "Can I go look at it again?"

I smiled and pushed my chair back to join him.

"Can I touch it?"

I laughed. "If you want to."

"I mean, I won't ruin it, will I?"

"No. It's dry. Touch away."

He picked the painting up by the edges and moved closer to the window. I stood behind him and studied the areas I hadn't been completely happy with, thrilled that they no longer bothered me.

Knox carried the painting back to the easel as though it would break apart in his hands if he wasn't careful. "Is it really for me?" he asked, coming back over to where I stood.

"It really is. If you want it."

He shook his head, smiled, and wrapped his arm around my waist. "I want to watch next time."

"Your wish, then, is granted since I planned to do a couple more this afternoon."

"You can do more than one in a day?"

"If I'm inspired."

Knox nuzzled my neck. "Did I inspire you?"

It was as playful and flirtatious as he'd been since he'd asked if anyone else in my family was artistic and I'd reacted so badly.

"Tara…"

"Knox…"

"I'm having really naughty thoughts."

"So am I."

He pulled back and looked into my eyes. "Do they involve you painting while naked?"

I might have laughed if I hadn't seen the heat in his eyes.

"I was thinking of painting you naked."

"*Jesus.*" I felt the shudder go through him at the same time he clenched my body tight to his. "That was so fucking sexy."

I reached up and kissed him, pressing my tongue between his parted lips.

"Do you know how hard it's been to keep my hands off you?" He murmured before bringing his lips back to mine and grasping the back of my neck to hold me still.

"I do," I whispered, reaching around to grab the cheeks of his tight ass. I shifted my body to grind against his hardness.

"Fuck," he groaned.

When he put his hands under my ass and lifted, I wrapped my arms around his neck and my legs around his waist. Our mouths stayed plastered together with every step up the staircase.

Knox stopped outside the bedroom door. "Are you ready for this, Tara?"

I thought for a split second about giving him a smart-ass response, as in, *I've been ready,* but Knox had had a good reason for us to wait, and I respected him for it.

"Please," I said instead.

He carried me over to the bed, set me on the mattress, and knelt in front of me. He painstakingly slowly unfastened the buttons of my blouse. When he finally reached the bottom, I shrugged the garment from my arms. Knox leaned forward and bit my nipple through the thin lace of my bra.

"God, I love your tits."

"Small," I muttered.

"Perfect." He reached around and unfastened the hooks. I shrugged until it fell away, leaving my breasts bare. He kissed each one and then looked up into my eyes. "Tara, I can't wait."

"I don't want to wait." I unfastened my pants, and he pulled them off my body. He lifted me under my arms until I was farther back on the bed, and spread my legs open.

23

Halo

I looked down at her glistening pussy while I tore the clothes from my body. I didn't care if they remained in one piece, and I sure as hell didn't care where they landed. Racing over to my bag, I grabbed a condom, tearing it open with my teeth. We had the rest of the day, the night, and as much time after that as we wanted, to take things slow. I'd linger over every inch of her body—later. Now, I had to be inside of her.

"Tara," I said again, needing her eyes to meet mine.

She reached for my cock; I smiled and moved her hand away. "Later, sweetheart." I positioned myself at her entrance and eased inside. "Are you ready for me, baby?"

"Yes," she mewled.

My eyes rolled back in my head when I felt how tight, wet, and warm she was. I stopped moving and looked into her deep blue eyes. I wanted to remember everything about this moment. I held myself above her with one arm and leaned down to kiss her. I didn't close my eyes, and neither did she. I loved that.

"God, you are so tight, so hot around me," I groaned as I began moving slowly at first, but soon couldn't hold back. I flipped Tara over, wrapped my arm around her waist, and pounded into her.

"Knox," she cried out as her pussy clenched around me. I pulled out and rolled to my back. "I want to watch you make yourself come on me."

Tara didn't hesitate. She straddled me, moving slowly at first but, like me, became frenzied when she couldn't hold back any longer. I clasped both her hands with mine and looked into her eyes. "Now, Tara," I groaned as I emptied myself into her.

She collapsed on my chest, both of us covered in a sheen of sweat, trying to catch our breath. I cupped her cheek with my hand, angled my neck, and captured her mouth with mine. Her touch was soft as she stroked my face with her fingertips.

"Look at me. Let me see those beautiful eyes. That gorgeous smile."

Tara shifted so she was tucked against my side. I turned to face her.

"You are amazing."

Her cheeks flushed, and I knew inside she wanted to deny it but knew I wouldn't let her.

"Don't move," I said, getting up to dispose of the condom and to make sure I had a couple more handy. When I returned, Tara was lying on her back, staring at the ceiling with a faraway look in her eyes. "Everything okay?"

She shook her head. "Everything is wonderful."

"You scared me for a second."

She rolled her eyes and her body toward me at the same time. "As if you have any doubt of your prowess."

I raised my eyebrows. "Prowess, eh?"

"You're a fantastic lover, Knox."

There was a time that those words would've brought me nothing but pride and pleasure. Not anymore. I wanted so much more than for her to think of me as "a lover." From this day on, I wanted to be her only lover. What would her reaction be if I admitted to it? Would she scoff? Act as though what had just happened between us didn't matter?

I'd confessed to thinking that once Tara and I got to know one another better, she'd realize she was way out of my league.

"Whatever you're thinking, you're wrong." She put one arm around my waist and rested her chin on my chest.

"Yeah? What if I was thinking that you were also a fantastic lover?"

"I'd say you were being generous."

I closed my eyes and took a deep breath. "Tara, you just rocked the fuck out of my world. So much so, that I'm trying my hardest not to ravish your body again, right this second. There is nothing generous about how much I want you. It's all greed. I want all of you, and I don't ever want any other man to have his hands on what I'm already claiming as mine."

I couldn't have stopped blabbering with the bit about rocking my world? Did I really have to keep going and probably scare the shit out of her by admitting I thought of her as mine? I opened my eyes, afraid her thoughts of horror were written on her face. Instead, she was smiling.

"Yours?"

"That's right. All mine."

"What about you? Do I get to claim you back?"

"You did the first time I saw you."

Tara and I made love for the rest of the afternoon. That's what it was. It wasn't fucking. It wasn't sex. It was making love to each other's bodies. Like so many other things I'd admitted to myself in the last few hours, I added another to it. I never dreamed I'd be the kind of guy who thought those words, let alone said them out loud. *Making love. Tara and I made love.* The more it repeated in my head, the better it sounded.

"What are you thinking now?" she asked, her chin resting on my chest again.

"That I want to make love to you all night." I waited for something to happen. Lightning bolt? Tara to laugh? Me to feel like an idiot as soon as I stopped talking? None of those things happened. Instead, Tara rested her cheek against my heart.

"I want to make love to you too, Knox. All night…"

"Why do I sense a 'but' coming?"

"But I'm really hungry."

We ate, we talked, we laughed, we made love all night, and the next morning, the farmhouse was still standing. The earth hadn't shattered, but every wall I'd unknowingly erected around my heart, had. I was captivated by Tara Emsworth.

A few days later, Agent Casavetti called to say he'd discovered more information regarding Richard Emsworth and asked if I could make arrangements to return to his office.

"You have to leave again?" Tara asked, biting her lip when I told her I'd be going back to Florence the next morning.

I cupped her cheek. "Are you going to miss me?"

"No. I mean, yes, but…"

I tightened the arm I had around her as we lay in bed. "But?"

"Ever since… the kidnapping. I get anxious."

I kissed the top of her head. "Completely understandable, but I assure you, you're safe here."

"We were supposed to be safe then too."

I'd heard about the mission that resulted in Tara, Aine McNamara, and Penelope Ramsey being kidnapped by a group of Armenians. I hadn't heard how the kidnappers got to them, and I wasn't sure now would be the right time to ask.

"Did you know I was also kidnapped?"

She looked up at me with wide eyes.

"I was in Somalia, undercover. Tackle was with me. A band of pirates thought we were their tickets to vast riches."

"What happened?"

"Striker brought a team in, and they rescued us."

"I thought they were going to kill us. I was sure of it," she said.

I put my finger on the bottom of her chin so she'd look at me. "I wish I had been there to keep you safe, Tara. I promise you now, though, you are. No one can get to you here."

"I wish I could say that makes me feel better, but it doesn't. Before I left New York, I was on medication for anxiety. I'm obviously not anymore."

"Would it help if you were?"

"I think so."

"I'll look into finding a doctor who can write you a prescription. In the meantime, I want you to remember that I left before. You were safe, and I came back. The same thing will happen tomorrow."

"I know you're right, but after seeing that man in Florence. I couldn't go through it again, Knox. I swear it would kill me even if the kidnappers didn't."

"It isn't going to happen again, Tara. Please try to trust that I won't allow it."

She nodded and rested her cheek against my heart. I waited for her to fall asleep before I allowed myself to drift off. At least, I hoped she was asleep.

When I arrived at the AISE field office the next day, Agent Casavetti told me additional victims had come forward to say the artwork they'd purchased via Richard Emsworth were verified to be forgeries.

"There are more victims of these crimes who will not come forward," he warned.

"You say that as though you know who some of them are."

Mateo opened a laptop and stood to turn off the lights in the room when a digital slideshow appeared on a screen on the other side of the room.

"The two Van Gogh pieces you see on the screen were discovered at a known member of the 'Ndrangheta crime syndicate's home. They were stolen over a decade ago." I had to admit that while I wasn't an art aficionado, I was certainly aware of the artist and his work. These were two paintings I'd never seen before.

The next photo that came on the screen was of thirteen different images. "The heist in which all of this artwork was stolen occurred over thirty years ago. One of the works was recently discovered when a construction crew began excavating a building known to be owned by a 'Ndrangheta boss."

"Where are you going with this, Agent Casavetti?"

"It seems there is a secret tradition of art theft among the crime families that goes back to the early twentieth century. As you know, Italy is the greatest artistic treasure house in Europe. Even the most hardened of criminal hearts can't help knowing the value of the art that surrounds us every day—even in the streets of our cities."

He was taking a long time to get to the point, but I saw where he was going.

"We have reason to believe the 'Ndrangheta is using stolen art as collateral or even currency in drug deals. Possession of artistic masterpieces is considered tremendous wealth. While it obviously cannot be sold through legal means, that is true of most everything that changes hands through the black market."

"Emsworth sold forged paintings to members of the 'Ndrangheta?"

"That is our belief, yes."

"Do you think he's still alive?"

"Most definitely."

"Tell me why, Mateo."

"Our sources believe they want the forger's head before they take his."

"Do your sources have any idea who the forger is?"

Casavetti nodded slowly. "They believe it is someone in his family."

"How closely related?"

"Very."

"Are you suggesting Emsworth's daughter is the forger?" The idea of it was ludicrous.

"Not necessarily."

I wondered how AISE solved a single crime. My experience was they were masters of innuendo in settings that called for the straightforward exchange of information.

When I left the meeting, the first call I made was to Tackle.

"I need your help with something."

"Shoot."

"Take a deeper look into her and her parents' background. I'm looking for possible siblings."

"Copy that. I'll get back to you with what I find."

My second call was to Striker. There were several organizations I wanted information from, and he'd be able to disseminate it more quickly than I could.

One thing that made no sense to me was why no one from the US had come forward saying they too purchased forgeries from Emsworth. News that he was a wanted man had certainly made the headlines. It stood to reason that many, particularly in New York City's social circles, would have fallen victim to his scam. Yet, there hadn't been a single one.

The victims were scattered across Europe, but that appeared to be it. No one had come forward from wealthier middle eastern countries, Russia, or China. In all of those cases, whether a single victim came forward or not, by now, the CIA would have gotten word of an international hunt for Emsworth. So why only Europe?

"An AISE informant believes the forger is someone close to Emsworth," I told Striker. "They believe there is a familial connection."

"We've run background—"

"Dig deeper. Nieces, nephews, cousins…" I ended the call before I could let my anger get the better of me. I needed something—anything—that would point toward someone other than Tara being the forger.

When I returned to the farmhouse, I found Tara outside, painting. There were several canvases lined up, resting against the low stone wall that surrounded the *terrazza*. Each looked as though she'd done a small amount of work and then abandoned them.

"What are these?" I asked after giving her a kiss that let her know being away from her for only a few hours was agony.

"I'm painting with oils today. I haven't for quite a while, so I need practice. Plus, they have to dry a bit before I do more."

The colors on the unfinished pieces were so different than her watercolors. They were darker, more like the Gothic work we'd seen at San Marcos.

"Oh, Pia came down earlier. She asked if I could work in the tasting room for a few hours once you returned from Florence."

I had research to do, but there was no reason I couldn't do it from the winery.

"Of course," I muttered, looking back at the unfinished paintings.

"Great. I'll just clean up."

It took over a half hour for Tara to "clean up," which was a grueling process, involving foul-smelling liquids.

"Is this stuff toxic?" I asked, studying the can that held the solution.

"Probably. It could be why so many of the masters eventually went mad. Although, today's dissolvents, I'm sure are more environmentally friendly."

"Environment? What about to humans?"

"I certainly wouldn't drink it."

"I'm not sure I'm a fan of oil painting."

Tara shrugged. "Every medium is fraught with something that makes the process difficult. I admit that when we were at the Accademia Gallery, I was inspired to paint the way people like da Milano, Michelangelo, and Cennino did. A challenge, if you will."

"Have you ever tried copying their work?"

She cocked her head. "It's not an uncommon practice for students." She pointed over to the *terrazza*. "That's what all those are."

"I thought you were an art history major."

Her eyes scrunched. "I was. I also took painting classes."

"What will you do with them?"

"Eventually, paint over them."

"Would you sell them?"

Tara's eyes widened. "Of course I wouldn't. What an odd question."

"If they're good enough, I would think there'd be a market for them."

"Not a legal one." She shook her head as though I was thick as a plank. Her words should reassure me, but that she was painting them at all, bothered me.

24

Tara

"You are not your usual happy self, at least since you've been staying at the farmhouse, Catarina."

I looked over at the table where Knox sat. He had the same scowl on his face he'd had since our strange conversation earlier. He was studying his laptop, periodically looking over in my direction, but when he did, he didn't smile.

"Ah, I see," said Pia, following my line of sight. "It is never easy, is it?"

"What do you mean?"

"Uomini difficili."

I laughed. "I'm sure they say the same about women."

Pia walked over to where the bottles of wine were stored and pulled one out. There was no one in the tasting room presently, but within thirty minutes, another tour bus was scheduled to arrive.

"I promised you a story about my friend Mylos."

"That's right," I said, taking a sip of the wine she poured. "Oh my God, that is so good," I groaned.

"I know." She smiled and motioned toward Knox with her head. "You two are so *sympatico*."

"Are we? There are times I wonder."

"Let me tell you about Mylos. To be honest with you, he is not my friend. Well, he is, but he is so much more."

"He must be someone very special."

"*Sì,* he is the man I will love until the day I die." She frowned. "I look out at the vineyards of Valentini, the place that isn't just my life, it's my heart, but Mylos… he is not here."

"Where is he?"

"That is a very long story. One that I will tell you now." She waved her hand at one of the stools at the tasting bar, and I sat down.

"We met when we were both sixteen years old. His family came from England to visit, and the first time I saw him, I swear to you, I fell in love." She smiled and leaned forward. "He was so handsome, like Ben, not as *molto muscoloso* as Ben, but still, *un uomo forte.* You understand what I mean, *sì?* "

"I do."

"His family had to leave suddenly that summer while I was away on a sales trip with my father. When I returned, I was heartbroken to find him gone. So much so that two years later, I did a crazy thing." She shook her head and laughed.

"What did you do?"

"I went to London to see him."

"That was crazy?"

"*Sì,* it was, because while I was in London, Mylos was here at Valentini."

"What happened?"

"On my last day there, he came home. We had only one wonderful night together. We talked all night long, kissing and laughing until the next morning when he had to take me to the airport."

"Is that the last time you saw him?"

"Oh no. Another two years passed, and we met again. It was then that Mylos and I finally made love. The time we had together was so brief, but if there had been any doubt in my mind that I loved him, after we were together, I knew it like I know my own hands." She held them out in front of her, turning her palms up and down. "When Mylos left, he was sent to Iraq, and there, the tank he was driving in hit an IED. You know what that is, *sì?* "

I put my hand in front of my mouth. "I do, and I'm so very sorry, Pia."

"Mylos did not die, Catarina, but he was very badly burned. His sister, Lily, contacted me and asked me to come to Germany to the burn hospital. When I did, he turned me away. Didn't want to see me."

The story she was telling me was so tragic, I was truly at a loss for words. I brushed the tear from the corner of my eye. "You never saw him again?"

"No, I did. Only once more. I cannot say that either of us ran away, Catarina, but we didn't run to each other either. Do you understand?"

"How long has it been?"

"One year."

"I'm sure—"

She held up her hand. "I need you to listen to me, Catarina. Learn from my heartbreak. Do not run away when love is within your reach."

I sat back in my chair. "Love? Don't be ridiculous, Pia. We hardly know each other."

"You are wrong. The heart knows when it finds its match. You and Ben are a match."

Based on what? He'd been hired to find me and now was looking for my father, a fugitive. If I knew where my father was, I wouldn't tell Knox. In fact, I'd do everything in my power to help my father stay hidden forever. He wasn't a bad man. He'd gotten himself involved in things I still knew very little about. What I did know, though, was that it was bad enough that he felt he'd had to run. Not just him, me too.

Knox and I still hadn't talked about him, and I knew that conversation was coming. I also knew that when it did, it would drive us further apart.

I turned to Pia, who was studying me.

"I think you should try to see Mylos again," I said.

"I don't know. When we were last together, we spent several days in each other's arms, making love, not seeing anyone but room service when they delivered our food."

"How did you leave things between you?"

"The injuries Mylos suffered were terribly painful, as you can imagine. During our time together, I discovered he was abusing his medication. He asked me to help him, and I did. The last time I saw him was outside of a rehab center in London."

"A year ago?"

"*Sì.*"

"Do you know if he's doing any better?"

"I think so. He's written a couple of letters, and I talk to Lily; that's his sister."

"I remember."

"I thought, after, that he'd come."

"Here?"

"*Sì.* I have gone to Mylos many times. More than I should have. I cannot continue to leave Valentini. I am not only responsible for the winery, Catarina. The fate of everyone who works for our family, even the estate itself, rests on my shoulders. My life is here. Mylos is not."

"Have you asked him to be?"

Pia rested her hand on my arm. "I am trying to help you with Ben, not have you help me with Mylos."

"Isn't that what friends do, Pia? Help each other?"

She hugged me. "I am so happy you are here, but something tells me you will not be much longer."

"I'm not sure."

"Whether you are or not, I want you to know that you will always be welcome here at Valentini."

"I appreciate that so much." I saw the tour bus pull up outside the tasting room window, and wiped away the tears I'd shed both at her story and her kindness. "Time to get back to work."

"One more thing I forgot to tell you. I have to be away from Valentini for a few days. I'm taking my mamma to Milan to see a specialist. I'm hoping he can figure out why she is so ill. We will close the winery to the public while I'm away."

Pia invited us to join her and her mother for dinner, but I politely declined. I'd been too stressed all afternoon, worrying about Knox's mood swings, and I wasn't hungry. It seemed that neither was he, since he didn't object when I said no, thank you.

When we got to the farmhouse, I went upstairs to change; Knox didn't follow. I hated the way I was feeling. It was as though he was angry with me about something, and I had no idea what.

I took a shower, hoping the hot water would lessen the tension in my shoulders. If anything, I felt worse once I got out, mainly because Knox hadn't come to see if he could join me. Finally, not being able to stand it any longer, I went downstairs in search of him.

"I don't like this," I blurted when I found him, still on his laptop, sitting at the table in the kitchen.

He looked up at me with wide eyes. "What don't you like?"

"If you're angry with me, just say so."

"I'm not angry with you, Tara."

"Then, why are you acting like you are?"

"It's a miracle we can both fit in this room with the size of the elephant. Don't you agree?"

"Are you talking about my father?"

"Don't you think it's time we did?"

"Why didn't you just say that?"

"You're right. I should have." He stood and pulled the cork out of the bottle of wine we'd opened the night before. "Want a glass?"

"No, thank you." I went and filled a pitcher of water instead, got two glasses from the cupboard, and set them on the table between us.

I folded my hands in front of me.

"I'm going to ask you this straight out."

"Go ahead."

"Do you know where your father is?"

"No."

"Do you have reason to believe he's in Italy?"

"Yes."

"Why?"

"Because it's where I was told he'd be."

"When?"

"The day I left New York."

"What else were you told?"

"What do you mean?"

"Do you know what crimes your father has been accused of?"

If I thought I hated the way Knox was acting toward me before, the way he was now made me loathe him. Couldn't he ask me these questions without sounding like he was interrogating me?

"No, Ben, I don't."

He sat back and glared at me. "What's that all about? Why'd you call me Ben?"

"Because you're acting like someone I don't know."

"I'm asking you questions, Tara. It shouldn't be a big deal for you to answer them, unless you have something to hide."

When I stood, I thought about slapping his face. Instead, I walked out of the room and went upstairs. This time, Knox followed.

"We aren't finished," he said as we approached the master bedroom.

"Yes. We are."

"You can't keep avoiding having this conversation."

"I can't? Or what? You'll arrest me?"

"Tara! What the hell?"

"Can't you hear yourself? You're treating me like a criminal."

"Are you?"

I spun around and grabbed the handle of the bedroom door. Before I could open it, Knox snaked his hand around my waist.

"Do you want to tell me one more time what you intend to do with all those paintings?"

"Let go of me."

"Answer me."

"Right now, I'd like to burn them."

"To get rid of the evidence?"

"You've gone crazy. I don't know what in the hell you're talking about. Now, please, let me go."

He did, but stayed on my heels. "Are you saying you have no idea why your father is on the run?"

I grabbed a bag and started tossing clothes into it.

"What are you doing?"

"I'm not staying here with you, Knox."

He folded his arms in front of him. "Going off to find your other boyfriend?"

I looked up at him with tear-filled eyes. "Why are you acting this way?"

"Because of your refusal to tell me the truth."

"What truth?"

"What do you really intend to do with those paintings, Tara?" He ran his hand through his hair. "Did you really think I was that stupid? That you could do it right in front of me?"

I sat on the end of the bed and stared at him. "I don't know what it is you think I've done, but this conversation, the way it's going now, needs to stop."

"I agree."

"You can either treat me with respect, and start at the beginning, or I'm leaving. As to where I'm going, it would be up to the villa to stay with Pia." As soon as the words left my mouth, I realized I couldn't do that. Pia was leaving in the morning to take her mother to Milan. I'd have to come up with another solution, and I had no idea what that might be, unless I could go back to the *casina*.

Knox walked over to the bedroom window and looked out. He stood there long enough without speaking that I wondered if he would.

"Your father has been indicted for wire fraud and enterprise corruption."

"I don't even know what that means."

"Art forgery, Tara. He's sold millions of dollars of fake art throughout Europe."

My head reeled with the weight of his words. So much so that I thought I might pass out. Everything Knox had asked me made so much more sense. "You think it was me," I whispered.

"I didn't want to."

"What do you mean?"

"I didn't think you had it in you. I honestly couldn't believe you were that kind of person."

"What changed your mind?"

"One of the paintings was recovered two days ago. That's why I was called to Florence."

He walked over to the closet and went inside. When he came back out, he had what looked like a painting wrapped in brown paper. He tore the wrap away and held it up. "Look familiar?"

I shook my head.

"Strange because the forensics team found a hair inside of the frame. A blonde hair. It wasn't long, but it was enough for them to run a DNA test. What do you think they found?"

"Tell me, Knox."

"Since they already had your father's DNA on file, it was easy for them to quickly determine whether it was a match. I got the results a few minutes ago. According to the test, there is a ninety-nine percent certainty that the person whose hair we found is Richard Emsworth's biological child."

"I see."

"I thought you might."

"What happens now? Do you arrest me?"

"Explain it to me. Why was your hair found inside the frame, Tara?"

The explanation was that the test had to be faulty. The hair wasn't mine, although I couldn't tell him whose it was, because I had no siblings. But until I talked to my father, I couldn't tell anyone that. Not even Knox.

"Tara?"

"I can't explain it."

Anger and frustration seeped out of every one of Knox's pores. "I want to help you, Tara, but until you tell me the truth, I can't."

Like before, when Knox stood silently at the window, neither of us spoke for long enough that I wondered if there was anything left for either of us to say.

"I'm going to sleep in the other room."

He nodded. "I think that's for the best."

I walked across the hallway, closed the other door behind me, and threw myself on the bed. This was no different than the message Penelope had left, accusing me of stealing money and jewelry from her, Aine, and Ava. Actually, it was different. That had been worse. They'd known me almost all my life. Knox didn't know me at all.

25

Halo

Honestly, what had I expected? That there would be some reasonable or even logical explanation of why her hair was found on a forged painting's frame?

I went back downstairs, wishing I had something stronger than wine to drink. It wouldn't matter if it were grain alcohol, though. Even the ninety-proof shit wouldn't numb the pain I felt.

Why had I been so certain Tara was "it" for me? Was it because I'd been so desperate after the plane crash to find someone to spend my life with that I turned a blind eye to the fact I didn't know her at all? She'd said it again and again. *I didn't know her.*

What a fucking jackass I was, thinking that Tara and I had been *making love.* It was a giant load of horseshit, and I'd climbed right in the middle of it like it was a field of daisies.

I went outside and called Tackle.

"Hey, man." He sounded groggy.

"It's the middle of the fucking afternoon; what are you doin'? Taking a nap?"

"What do you want, Knox?"

"Tara Emsworth is the art forger. This whole time, her little-miss-innocent, serious-lack-of-self-esteem bullshit was all an act."

"Hang on a sec."

I heard rustling in the background, like he had been sleeping. After the sound of two doors closing, he said, "Okay. Start over."

"Richard Emsworth is wanted for selling forged art. Millions of dollars worth."

"I know that part."

"Tara was the one painting the forgeries."

"Are you sure?"

"They recovered one and, lo and behold, inside of the frame, they found a hair. DNA matched daddio's."

"It couldn't have been his?"

"It wasn't one hundred percent. If it had been, yes, it could've been his. Instead, it means it belongs to one of his children."

"And Tara's the only one?"

"Unless you've found another."

"Sorry, man. I haven't."

"I'm grasping at straws. She doesn't have any brothers or sisters. Said so herself. The only way it wouldn't be hers is if it belonged to her sibling. Those are the facts."

"I couldn't find any record of Tara's mother giving birth to another child."

Tara's mother? What about her father? Harder to track if he'd had any other children, but there were ways.

"Let's try another tack."

"What's that?"

"Half brothers or sisters on her father's side."

"Give me a few hours, and I'll see what I can dig up. In the meantime, try not to say anything to her that you can't take back."

Tackle ended the call before I could tell him it was way too late for that.

The next morning, I rewrapped the painting to return it to Agent Casavetti's office. The door to the bedroom where Tara was sleeping hadn't opened, and I doubted it would until after she was sure I'd left.

I thought about doing so without saying anything, but Tackle's words replayed in my head. Instead of walking out the front door, I ran back upstairs.

"Tara?" I called out, knocking.

"What do you want, Knox?"

"I need to talk to you before I leave." I tried the knob, but the door was locked.

"Hang on," she said, opening it seconds later.

"Hi." I wanted to reach out, pull her into my arms, and tell her I knew it had to be a mistake, that I'd been wrong last night. I even wanted to pretend none of it had happened. There hadn't been a hair. Or even a painting recovered. That there hadn't been a DNA match.

Her eyes were swollen from crying, and she looked like she hadn't gotten any more sleep than I had. Behind her, I saw her bags were packed.

"I have to go into Florence, but when I get back, I'll talk with Pia about you staying in the villa."

"That won't be necessary."

"What do you mean?"

"I'm going home. Back to America."

I leaned against the doorjamb. "When did this come about?"

"I called Quinn last night. She's making the arrangements with her dad today. I'm sure you'll hear something directly from him."

I turned to walk away but looked back at her. "Tara, can you tell me I'm wrong? Can you give me any explanation for why your hair was found in the painting?"

Her deep blue eyes flooded with tears, and she turned away from me. "I cannot."

Once in the car, I checked the time. It was one in the morning in California. I'd likely hear from Doc later, after he made arrangements for Tara to travel back to the States. If he'd let me, I wanted to go with her. Even if she didn't want me around, I'd be there. I'd stay quietly by her side, through whatever she faced. There was a good chance that if she gave up her father, she'd get a deal and not have to serve jail time. I had no doubt Doc would work hard on her behalf to see to it that it went down exactly that way.

Memories of my dad flashed in my mind. "Even if it seems insurmountable, we will always be there for you, Knox. We will always do everything in our power to help you get through whatever obstacles you face."

I hated leaving Tara right now. So much that I thought about racing back upstairs, repeating my promise to help her, and taking her with me to Florence, just so I could have her in my sight.

I couldn't do that, though. She didn't trust me, not that she had reason to. Even if I swore I wasn't taking her into custody, she wouldn't buy it.

I started the engine, telling myself that the faster I got to Florence, the sooner I'd be back.

I was about to walk out of my meeting with Agent Casavetti when both of our cell phones rang. At the same time, someone ran toward us in the hallway.

"There's been a shooting at Valentini. Two agents are down!" the man shouted.

"I'm calling Lucia," Mateo said, hitting the screen of his phone with the tip of his finger. *"Quello che è successo?"* he shouted when she answered. "Wait. I'm putting you on speaker."

"Mancuso is down, so is Romano." It sounded as though she was running.

"What about Tara?" I asked.

"I don't know yet."

"Where is Pia?" asked Mateo.

"She and her mother are in Milano. They left early this morning."

"Confirm that," Mateo said to me.

I stepped away and dialed Pia, who immediately answered. "Hello, Ben. How are you this morning?"

"I'm fine, Pia. Thanks. Um, did you happen to speak with Tara this morning?"

"Tara?"

"I'm sorry. Catarina."

"No, my mamma and I left very early. Is everything okay?"

"Yes, everything is fine."

"Ben? You're worrying me."

"She and I had a spat, is all."

"I see. I warned you not to hurt our Catarina."

"I'll do my best to make it up to her. I promise. I've got to go. Oh, before you hang up, when do you think you'll return?"

"Not for a few days. I told Catarina this yesterday. I'm taking my mamma to see a medical specialist. Is there a reason I need to come back?"

"No, of course not. I'm sorry to have bothered you with this."

I relayed everything I'd learned from Pia to Mateo as we raced out of the building. Not far from where we stood, a helicopter waited to transport us to Valentini. We were inside, headsets on, when another call came through from Lucia. Mateo hung his head as he listened.

"Both Mancuso and Romano are dead. Tara Emsworth is nowhere to be found."

Once back at Valentini, I couldn't control the thoughts racing through my head. There wasn't a single part of me that believed Tara killed two AISE agents. Imagining what might have happened instead, left me feeling so sick to my stomach that I'd attempted emptying it more than once.

I watched from the *terrazza* as a team from AISE continued to comb the farmhouse for evidence. Other than the fact that the two men assigned to her detail were dead, there was no other sign of a struggle.

I checked the time. It had been seven hours since the call came in, saying the two agents were down. Seven hours since I called Doc to brief him on what had transpired and tell him that Tara was, again, missing.

It would be another eight before he and whomever he was bringing from the K19 team landed at the Florence airport. The only person I knew for certain was coming, other than him, was Tackle. Doc made it clear that when the K19 plane stopped at the private airfield near JFK to refuel, Tackle would meet them there.

"Wait," I'd said before he ended the call. "I'm sorry, Doc."

"Apology not accepted. You've nothing to be sorry for."

Whatever the ultimate outcome, I'd handled so many things wrong since the day I first set foot in Italy that I didn't deserve to become a K19 partner. Security guard at a mall would be out of my reach.

Mateo was the lead on the investigation into Tara's disappearance and the death of the agents. Initially, he'd deferred to me, but I told him I was standing down.

"We're checking in with informants and running as much security footage as we can," he reported. "So far, nothing."

It was just after one in the morning when Doc, Tackle, Striker Ellis, and Razor Sharp walked into the farmhouse on the Valentini estate. Mateo Casavetti and the rest of his team had left a little after ten, promising to be back at eight the next morning.

"There's another vehicle behind us," said Doc, stepping aside to let Tackle greet me first.

"How are you holding up?"

"I fucked up big-time, man," I mumbled, turning my back to the other two guys.

The front door opened again. Gunner Godet and Mercer Bryant, along with his wife, Quinn, Razor's wife, Ava, Aine McNamara, and Penelope Ramsey walked in.

"I don't know about the other two, but both Ava and Quinn threatened their husbands with divorce if they couldn't come along," said Tackle, who stepped aside as, one by one, the four women hugged me.

"Have a seat, Halo," said Doc. "We'll bring you up to speed on what we've learned."

The last thing I wanted to do was sit, but I followed Doc's orders anyway.

"Two things," said Razor. "First, we have reason to believe Tara was taken by men working for the 'Ndrangheta crime syndicate." He looked over at Ava, who was crying.

"I'm sorry," she said. "I'm okay. Go on."

He sighed. "They've all been briefed," he said to me. "This isn't news to them."

I nodded. "Is there more?"

He tossed a couple of grainy photos down in front of me. One image made me feel more nauseous than I had in my life. It was of Tara, being carried into a building, blindfolded, bound, gagged, and more than likely drugged.

"Is this her father?" I asked, pointing to the photo of a man who appeared badly beaten. The question I wanted to ask, I wouldn't. Not with Tara's four best friends in the room.

"Tackle?" said Doc.

My friend stood, picked up his laptop, and sat beside me. "Your hunch about the half-sibling was dead-on, Halo. Tara doesn't have any full brothers or sisters, but her father did have a child with another woman before he married Tara's mother. My guess is he kept that kid's mom and maybe even the kid himself, paid off for years. He doesn't go by Emsworth. The name is Brando Ripa."

Tackle opened several images on the screen. "This was taken a few years ago when he graduated from the Art Institute of Chicago. Before you ask, it is known more for being a museum, but there is a college attached to it. They call it the School of AIC. It's considered one of the best art colleges in the world."

He moved the image on the screen so it was side by side with the one I took of the man I saw with Tara in the *casina.* It was impossible to tell for sure, but it could be the same guy.

"He left the States shortly after college and took up residence in Europe."

"You think he's the forger?"

Tackle nodded. "Not only that, I'm not entirely certain that Papa Emsworth knew what his son was up to."

He opened another document that looked like a bill of sale. "This lists four of the paintings that were reported to be forgeries." It was easy to see that Richard Emsworth had paid a hefty price for the originals. "There's provenance included with the invoice for every one of the pieces of art. We have more of these that also show provenance."

"We need to get on the move if we wanna get in and out before daylight," said Gunner, motioning with his head.

"Halo, the choice is yours. Stay or go," said Doc. "Either way, every one of us will back your decision."

"Go," I answered without hesitation. There was no fucking way I could stay here while the rest of the team attempted to clean up my mess. The other thing was, if it came down to it, I wouldn't hesitate for a split second to give my life to save Tara's.

"Eighty-eight, Razor, you'll stay here. Relay as much as you can find out about Ripa. Everyone else, gear is in the vehicles. Suit up. AISE is sending a team to meet us."

We were close to Florence, on the outskirts of where AISE's informant had said Tara and her father were being held in an abandoned warehouse, when I finally got the balls to ask. "Tara?"

Gunner, who was in the front passenger seat, turned and looked back at me. "First of all, we don't think the 'Ndrangheta family believes Tara had anything to do with this. What we do think is that the father is refusing to give up the whereabouts of the son."

"And Tara will?"

Gunner shook his head. "Daddy will pick her over him."

"And then what?"

"We get there first."

26

Halo

"Well, looky there," said Gunner through my earpiece. "One o'clock from the building's entrance, boys. Head 'em off."

Through my night-vision goggles, I got a clear read on the man I'd seen with Tara, being led from a vehicle toward the warehouse where she and her dad were being held.

"Stand down," said Gunner when I took a step forward. "Follow my lead."

I watched as the two men escorting Brando Ripa dropped to the ground after being taken out by a bullet, one each, in the head. Before their captive could flee, Doc, Striker, and two AISE agents grabbed him and pulled him into a waiting SUV.

"We're up," said Gunner, motioning for me to follow. "You know what to do?"

"Affirmative."

The handheld radar device AISE employed indicated there were six people inside the building. Which meant with four of us along with six from AISE, the 'Ndrangheta who were guarding Tara and her father were greatly outnumbered.

I had one job. Get in. Get Tara. Get out. No matter what else was going down, I was not to engage. Tackle's job was to get Tara's father.

"Get your asset and get the fuck out," Gunner repeatedly barked at us. "Nothing else. Do you understand me?"

"Copy that," I muttered.

"Let the big boys take care of the dirty work." I swear I saw him rub his hands together.

Seconds before we entered the building, the power was cut. "There!" Gunner said through the earpiece, pointing toward a body prone on a mattress on the floor. I raced over and gathered Tara into my arms, shielding her with my body as shots rang out all around us. There were more in the building than AISE had originally counted, but it wasn't up to me to cover the rest of the team. My job was to get Tara out. That was it.

I raced out the door into another waiting SUV. Lucia was behind the wheel. As soon as I had Tara inside with the door closed behind me, she sped from the building.

"She's breathing. Doesn't appear to have any visible injuries," I said, untying the ropes binding her. Once I freed her arms and legs, I removed the piece of cloth they used as a gag and then the blindfold. I cradled her in my arms, stroking her hair.

"We need to take her to a hospital," I said to Lucia, whose eyes met mine in the rearview mirror.

"I don't think that would be wise."

"She was obviously drugged with something."

Tara's eyes opened suddenly, and she thrashed against me. While I'd removed my helmet and face shield, the tactical gear I still wore must've frightened her.

I held her arms when she tried to hit me. "Shh, I've got you. You're safe now, Tara."

While I'd thought she was awake, it appeared more now that she was caught somewhere between the states of sleep and consciousness. She continued to struggle, trying to hit me and yelling to let her go.

"Tara, it's Knox! Wake up!" I shouted. She stopped moving, and her eyes studied me.

"You kidnapped me!"

I kept my grip tight on her wrists as much to stop her from hurting herself as me. "I rescued you."

"The last thing I remember…" She closed her eyes tight and then dissolved into sobs. *"You promised I'd be safe. You promised no one would get to me."*

Her biggest fear, the source of constant anxiety, I'd let happen. I knew better than to make promises I couldn't keep. Wanting to reassure her had led me to break another cardinal rule of the kind of work I did.

"It would be better not to go to the hospital," said Lucia. "AISE has a medical team who can check her out."

I nodded at her reflection in the mirror.

"They will meet us at Valentini."

A few minutes later, Tara tried to sit up, but I kept her tucked in my arms. "Where are we?" she asked.

"Outside of Florence." I wanted to ask Lucia about Richard Emsworth, if he would be brought to Valentini as well, but didn't. Given the way he looked in the photos I'd seen, I expected the medical treatment he'd need would be significantly more than Tara.

"I'm going to tell you what happened now, only because there are people waiting for you back at the farmhouse."

Her body, already tense, tightened more. "People?"

"People who love you."

"Pia?"

"Ava, Aine, Quinn, and Penelope."

Her eyes opened wide. "They're here?"

"They are."

"Knox, please let me sit up."

Since she no longer appeared to be struggling, I let her but kept my arm around her shoulders and held one of her hands in mine.

"Why did they come?"

"I contacted Doc from Florence when I got word of your kidnapping. He immediately got a team in the air, himself included, to come to Italy to find you. That team included Razor, Gunner, Mercer, and Tackle." When she didn't speak, I continued. "According to Tackle, two of your friends threatened their husbands with divorce unless all four of them could come along."

I saw a glimmer of a smile. "Sounds like them," she murmured.

"There's more I need to tell you."

Tara closed her eyes. "Okay."

"The men who kidnapped you were looking for your brother."

"My *what*?"

"I know about Brando, Tara."

"Brand isn't my brother."

"Half brother."

Tara shook her head. "No. You're wrong. He's my father's secretary's son." Her eyes opened wide when the truth dawned on her. *"Oh my God,"* she cried, putting her head in her hands. "Why were they looking for Brand?"

"From what we've been able to piece together, he was the one forging the paintings. It appears your father was unaware he was doing it until shortly before he was charged."

Her eyes opened, and she looked into mine. "Do you have proof?" she whispered.

"We'll know more once we're back at the farmhouse."

"Where's my dad?"

"He was being held at the same place you were taken."

"I don't remember any of it…after the farmhouse." She looked out the window and then back at me. "There are things you're not telling me."

I took a deep breath and let it out slowly. "Your father suffered injuries. I don't know to what extent yet, which is why I wasn't going to tell you."

"But he's alive?"

"Yes."

"What about Brand?"

My eyes met Lucia's, and she nodded.

"My understanding is that he's been taken into custody."

"You found him."

"The same people who found you, found him."

She took her hand from mine and laced her fingers with those of her other hand and looked out the window.

"Tara, I—"

She shook her head. "I can't take any more right now."

"How are you feeling?" I asked.

"I have a headache. Is there any water?" she asked without looking at me.

Lucia held up a bottle that I took and gave to Tara.

She didn't say anything else for the rest of the drive to Valentini. When we arrived, her four friends raced out the door of the farmhouse. Knowing they had her if she was weak, I got out the opposite door and went inside where Razor and Mercer were waiting.

Razor put his hand on my shoulder, and Mercer patted my back. "Job well done, Halo."

I couldn't disagree more, but there'd be plenty of time for us to talk about that later. I had no doubt there'd be a hotwash once we were back in the States, if not before.

"Have you heard anything about Emsworth's condition?"

"He was transported to a hospital outside Florence. They banged him up pretty good, but the worst of it was a few broken bones," said Razor.

"And the brother?"

"Doc is working that now."

"What does that mean?"

Razor looked at Mercer. "If they keep him in Italy, he'll be a dead man inside of a week."

"The 'Ndrangheta's arms reach well into the US," I said.

"They do, but we've got better control over where he ends up."

I didn't know whether K19 did or not, but that didn't necessarily matter to me. Tara mattered, and I'd fucked things up with her so bad, I doubted there'd be any coming back from it.

When I heard them coming inside, I went upstairs to the bedroom she and I had shared—where we'd made love. Whether she wanted anything to do with me or not, that's the way I'd remember our time together. We'd made love. No matter how hard I tried to tell myself I was an idiot for thinking I loved her, I did.

There was a knock at the door, and I walked over to open it. I hesitated for a moment, saying a silent prayer that it was Tara. It wasn't.

"Hey, Penelope."

She stepped forward and opened her arms. "Let me hug you."

"Sure," I mumbled. A hug would feel pretty damn good right now, even if it wasn't from the right woman.

"Thank you for all you've done for Tara."

I shook my head. "I don't know what it is you think I did."

"You saved her life."

"The credit for that goes to the entire K19 team."

"Not from the kidnapping. You saved her before that."

"She saved herself."

"She's mad at you right now, but she'll get over it."

"I'm really glad you all came. She needs you." I took a step back to close the door.

"She needs you too," she said right before it latched.

After locking the door, I went to the bed and stretched out on my back, hoping I could get some sleep. I'd drifted off when I heard another knock.

"Yeah?" I called out, wishing I could tell whoever it was to fuck off and leave me alone.

"Need you to come downstairs, Halo. Doc wants everybody in on this," said Mercer.

"Be right there."

I went into the bathroom and splashed my face with cold water. When I got to the bottom of the stairs, my eyes met Tara's. Too fast, she looked away.

I walked toward the kitchen and stood with my back against the wall so I could see her, but for Tara to see me, she'd have to turn around.

Ava and Aine sat on either side of her. Penelope and Quinn were sitting on the floor at Tara's feet. Each of her friends either had a hand on her or part of their body resting against hers. As much as I wished I was the one sitting beside her, that she was surrounded by so much love, warmed my ice-cold heart.

"We'll be here until Richard Emsworth is cleared for travel. I'm hoping that will be later today or tomorrow."

As he spoke, Doc glanced at Tara several times. I looked around the room and realized that neither Gunner nor Tackle was here.

"As far as Brando Ripa is concerned, since he's an American citizen, we've been able to make arrangements to extradite him back to the States."

"Where is he now?" I asked.

"Somewhere safe."

"The sooner we're all out of Italy, the better," said Razor.

Doc leveled his gaze at him and looked over at Tara again. "We have no intention of informing the owners of the Valentini estate of the events that took place here yesterday. AISE is on board with that."

"Copy that," I muttered.

"That's all for now." When he stopped talking, Doc walked in my direction. I followed him out to the *terrazza*.

"Gunner, Striker, and Tackle are with Ripa."

"Doing what?"

"'Recovering the originals.'"

"Where are they?"

"Closer than you think."

"Meaning?"

"He's saying that he hid them in the wine caves here on the estate."

"What happens next?"

"If Ripa is telling the truth and the originals are here, hidden at Valentini, then we have Emsworth's permission to make a deal with the 'Ndrangheta."

"To do what?"

"Give them something more valuable than what they lost."

"The originals?"

"For the forged painting sold to the don. If necessary, two. You know Gunner, he won't let them get away with more than that."

"What's going to happen to him?"

"Ripa?" Doc rubbed the back of his neck with his hand; I'd known him long enough to recognize his tell. "Less than probably should."

"Meaning?"

"If he makes restitution to the remaining victims, it's likely he won't get as much jail time."

"Does he have the money to do that?"

"We'll see, but my guess is that Richard Emsworth will figure out a way to get as much of it to go away as possible."

"I saw them together. Tara cares about him. I don't think she knew he was her brother, though."

Doc nodded and walked back inside.

27

Tara

"How are you feeling?" Quinn asked.

Heartbroken. "Fine."

"Headache?" asked Aine.

"Pretty much gone."

"Are you hungry?" Ava asked.

"Not really."

"Sad?" asked Pen.

She was the only one of the four who I looked up at. When my eyes met hers, I didn't see any sign that she was making fun of me. All I saw was love.

"Yeah."

Of the five of us, Ava and Aine were closest just because they were sisters. Quinn had always been closer to Aine than to the rest of us, and Pen and I, we were as close to sisters as it got, without the biology. We fought like sisters, but we had each other's backs in the same way Ava and Aine always had. That's why it had hurt so much when it was Pen who called to accuse me of stealing from them.

"Can you come with me for a minute?" she asked.

I stood and followed her up the stairs. "This is the room I was staying in," I said when she walked past it.

"That's the room your stuff is in." She walked straight into the master bedroom and sat on the end of the bed. "Come here, girlfriend."

When I sat down, she put her arm around my shoulders.

"Pen…"

"Cry it out, Tara."

I rested my head on her shoulder and cried as hard as I had when Knox held me in the SUV. This time, though, it was him I was sobbing over.

"Why don't you try to get some rest?" she said a few minutes later as I wiped my tears. "I'll stay."

I scooted up the bed and rested my head on the pillow Knox used. I fell asleep with my arms wrapped around it.

I woke when I heard Pen talking to someone. When I opened my eyes, I saw her and Knox standing in the doorway. I watched as she eased around him.

I sat up. "I was just leaving."

"Stay where you are," he said, coming over to sit beside me. "Look, earlier you stopped me from saying this, but I need to. I'm sorry, Tara."

"What for?"

"Doubting you. Among other things."

"You more than doubted me, Knox. What you accused me of was way beyond that. You thought I was an art forger." When he started to speak, I held up my hand. "You said you couldn't believe I thought you were so stupid, I did it right in front of you. Not only that, when I said I wanted to leave, you accused me of being with another man. I don't think there's much you didn't blame me for."

He hung his head. "I'm sorry. I don't know what else to say."

"Nothing else is necessary. You didn't—don't— know me well enough to believe otherwise. You were out to catch a criminal, and you did. Eventually. And just so you know, I was blindsided by all of this. All I knew was that my father had disappeared, and I wanted to find him."

"Is that why you came to Italy?"

"Is this another interrogation?"

Knox's eyes opened wide. *"Fuck,"* he muttered under his breath. "No. And I'm sorry. Again. I'm trying to piece it all together, and I have no reason to."

"Because you still think I'm guilty of something."

"No. Not at all."

"Right."

When I walked out of the room, the front door opened and my father walked in. "Daddy?" I flew down the steps, stopping just short of throwing my arms around him.

"Tara!" He held out one hand, I took it, and he pulled me in to hug him.

He looked like he'd been to hell and back, and to a certain extent, he had.

"I don't want to hurt you."

"You're here and safe," he said, stroking my hair. "I'm sorry for getting you mixed up in this."

"You didn't. I did."

"We can talk about all of this later."

I was about to nod but stopped myself. "No, Dad. There are things we need to talk about now."

While my father didn't look surprised, my four best friends certainly did.

There was no way my father could walk much farther than the nearest chair, so everyone else would have to leave. "Can you please excuse us?" I asked, looking around the room.

Lucia and the man who'd helped my father inside, escorted him to the chair where I pointed. Once he was seated, they stood behind him.

"Is my father under arrest?"

"No, but—"

"Please excuse us, then."

They followed the others who had been in the room out the door that led from the farmhouse to the *terrazza*.

Once I heard it close, I sat on the floor at my father's feet. He reached out and stroked my hair.

"I was so worried about you."

He closed his eyes and leaned his head against the back of the chair. "I'm sorry, Tara. For everything."

"I don't understand why you didn't just tell me. I've known Brand my whole life."

"It was Vi's decision, and I respected that."

"No one knew?"

My father shook his head. "No one."

"Did Brand know?"

"Eventually. Not until he was an adult."

"How did he find out? Did you tell him?"

"I set up a trust on his behalf, the same as what you have. When he turned twenty-five, the money became his. It was then that Vi decided it was time for him to know."

I thought back on that time. Brand had just graduated from college with his master's degree. I'd flown to Chicago to celebrate with him. Instead of a group dinner, Brand had asked me if he and I could go out alone. A part of me worried he thought there might be more than a friendship between us, but that hadn't been the case.

He told me that night that he was moving to Europe to pursue his art. I remembered being happy for him, but he didn't seem like he was for himself.

"It was right after his graduation," I murmured.

"That's right."

"He and I had dinner that night."

My father raised his eyebrows.

"I'd flown in to surprise him, thinking I'd just join in on whatever celebration was taking place. As it turned out, he was saying goodbye. He left for Italy a few days after that."

"Brand contacted me about a year later, asking if I'd help him get an art dealing business off the ground. It wasn't money he needed as much as my contacts, he'd said at the time."

"But you gave him money anyway?"

I knew how much money was in my trust fund, and my dad said Brand's was the same as what I had. He definitely wouldn't have needed cash.

"I offered to go into business with him instead." My dad hung his head. "Originally, I'd planned to ask you to come on board too, basically to do the same thing he was doing here—what I believed he was doing."

"Why didn't you?"

"Brand refused."

My first reaction was to be hurt, but I quickly realized that, instead, he'd been protecting me.

"He wanted to ruin you," I mumbled.

"Hurt me at the very least."

"I'm sorry, Dad."

"You have nothing to be sorry for, sweetheart."

"I'm just sorry any of it happened. I'm sorry Brand felt…" I shook my head. I had no idea what Brand thought or felt.

"I have a question for you."

I looked up at him.

"What made you come to Italy?"

"Vi. I'd been trying to reach you. It was Mom who suggested I ask her. She told me you'd gone to Italy and that you'd disappeared. She also told me Brand would help me find you. She was so worried." I bit my bottom lip, unsure whether I should ask anything else. "What happened?"

"I was on my way out of the airport in Florence when 'Ndrangheta henchmen picked me up. My plan had been to find Brand." My dad shook his head. "I thought the paintings I'd purchased were the forgeries. Since they were in Italy, I believed if I could go back to the dealers with them, I could prove I'd been duped as well. Evidently, they knew more than I did about the real story. They wanted me to hand over Brand."

"When was this?"

"The day before Thanksgiving."

I looked up when I heard a noise and saw Knox coming down the stairs.

He had a bag and a cardboard tube in his hands. "Can I talk to you for a minute?" he asked.

"I'm in the middle of something."

"It'll be quick, but it's urgent."

I followed him out the front door.

"How are you feeling?"

"That's urgent?"

He hung his head. "No. I'm sorry. Listen, I got an urgent call from my sister, um, Sloane."

"I remember."

"There's something going on at home. It was hard for me to hear her. Anyway, she asked—begged—me to come back to the States as soon as I can."

"Then, you should go."

"I hate leaving you, Tara."

"Because your being here kept me safe?" I saw him flinch and regretted the words as soon as I said them. "I'm sorry."

"Don't be. I deserved that." His voice was clipped, but in the same way he didn't know me well enough not to doubt me, I didn't know him well enough to know if he was hurt or angry.

He held up the tube. "I wanted to ask…You don't have to say yes, but the painting. Can I still have it?"

"It's yours, Knox. I painted it for you."

"Thank you." He looked up at the sky and then back at me. "There's so much—"

I shook my head. "There's nothing."

"Tara, I care about you. More than that."

I put my hand on the door. "Don't do this. Don't embarrass yourself further. Goodbye, Knox."

"Wow. Okay. I guess this is goodbye, Tara."

I stepped inside, closed the door behind me, and went back to where my father sat. From the window, I could see Knox studying the farmhouse. It was as though he was taking one last look at a place he'd never see again.

I'd hurt him with my cruelty. While part of me wanted to race outside and beg his forgiveness, another part knew it was pointless. We were from two very different worlds. How many times had I thought that once

Knox got to know me better, he'd realize I wasn't as interesting as he thought? He'd said that I'd figure out I was way out of his league.

He was so wrong; it was the opposite. Knox was one of the good guys. People like Ava and Aine, Quinn, and even Penelope deserved the good guys. I didn't. I was a spoiled rich girl whose daddy took care of my every material need and want. I'd graduated from college, but the first real job I'd had was the few days I worked with Pia in the winery tasting room.

I thought back to what Knox had told me his friend said. They'd survived a plane crash; they should go out and grab every bit of happiness they could.

Well, I'd survived two kidnappings. Instead of grabbing happiness, I had to make a life for myself where I could be happy. Be fulfilled. Find a way to be more than I was, so the next time I met one of the good guys, maybe I'd believe I deserved to be with him.

It was too late for Knox and me. In the short time we were together, we'd seen as much of the worst in each as we had the best.

I'd never forget him, though, and I hoped he'd never forget me. That's why I wanted him to take the painting. Something to remember me by. Something I was good enough at that he'd admired me for it.

I brushed away my tears as I watched Knox drive away.

"Sweetheart?" My father held his hand out to me.

"It's okay, Daddy." I sat on the floor and rested against his leg. He stroked my hair.

"What are you thinking about?" he asked a few minutes later.

"All the things I want to do with my life now that I've finally woken up enough to realize what's possible."

"Everything is possible. You're extraordinary, Tara."

I smiled up at him. "You're the only one who's ever thought so." That wasn't exactly true. There'd been a time Knox thought I was extraordinary too.

28

Tara
Three months later

"Knock, knock."

"You can come in, Pen."

"Oh my God, I love it. Even more than the last one." She spun around and looked at the row of paintings that were lined up against the far wall of my studio. "I don't know, it's too hard to decide. I love them all equally."

I smiled and hugged her, being careful not to drip paint on her shirt. "You don't, but I appreciate your support anyway."

"All those years, and we never knew how talented you were."

I shrugged. It was more that they'd never known how much I lacked enough confidence to share my work. The only person I had shown, before Knox, was Brand.

While Penelope studied the paintings, I thought about the man who I now knew was my half brother.

Thanks to my dad, restitution was made to all the people who had purchased forgeries from Brand or bought fake shares in masterpieces. I wondered if the money to do so came out of the trust fund or if my father had simply paid it all. Either way, it was none of my business, and I'd never ask.

Quinn was the one to tell me that Brand had been sentenced to six years in prison for his crimes, even after the restitution was made. It didn't seem nearly enough, but as she'd explained, Brand wasn't the one who'd kidnapped my father or me. He also hadn't been the one to kill the AISE agents who were protecting me. While, to some, it may seem that he should pay for the indirect consequences of his actions, as Quinn said, it wasn't the way the law worked.

I found myself intrigued by the original idea of the business Brand and my father had started, and quietly opened a retail space of my own. I'd named it the Catarina Benedetto Fine Art Collection and Gallery. It was only one of the businesses intended to operate under the umbrella of the Tribe of Five Corporation, whose board members included Quinn Bryant, Ava

McNamara, Aine Ellis, and Penelope Ramsey. We'd voted four to one to make Quinn our chairwoman.

I hadn't sold any of my own art yet and, secretly, wasn't sure I ever would. However, the gallery was beginning to gain in reputation for selling quality Italian works of art.

My plan was never to conduct any private art deals, but the market segment was growing quickly as savvy collectors, corporations, and even institutions like museums, began to realize the benefit of brokering one-on-one deals rather than competing in the sometimes overwhelming world of public galleries, high-end auctions, online sales, and art fairs. When initially approached about brokering a deal, I'd been reluctant, but now had finalized close to twenty.

Some dealers were hesitant to do business with me, given the level of provenance I required for any artwork I brokered in a deal. I was intransigent in insisting my requirements be met before I would continue the sale. Not that I was the face of that part of the business. That was Penelope.

While she'd loved physical therapy, the long hours and difficulty getting time off resulted in her asking if there was a place for her at the gallery.

"I've decided. This is my favorite." She stepped back and waved her hand at a painting of the Valentini Winery with rolling hillsides covered in vineyards in the background. I had to admit, it was one of my favorites too.

Pen walked over and sat on a stool by the window. "I have a crazy idea."

The way she said it, reminded me so much of Pia that I put my hand on my heart and my eyes filled with tears.

"What?"

"It's nothing. Just missing a friend."

"That's something else I want to talk to you about, but first things first."

"It isn't who you're thinking," I muttered.

"Don't try to distract me."

I folded my arms.

"It's time you mounted a show."

I shook my head. "No. Absolutely not."

"Why not? Look at all of this. How many paintings do you have now? Thirty? Forty?"

It was closer to fifty, none of which I was ready for anyone besides Pen to see. I would've let the remaining three of the tribe see them, but Quinn lived in

California and Ava in Oregon. I wasn't sure whether Aine and her husband, also one of the K19 Security Solutions partners, had made a decision about where they planned to live full-time. The last I heard, they were leaning heavily toward Yachats, the town on the Oregon Coast where Ava and Razor lived.

When we heard the chime of someone at the intercom at the front of the gallery, Pen eased out the door of my studio. "This conversation isn't over," she said before closing it behind her.

No sooner was she gone than my cell phone rang. "Hi, Daddy."

"Hey, princess. How are you?"

"Busy painting. How are you?"

"That's what I like to hear. I'm hoping someday you'll let me see some of them."

"I'll let you know."

"I wanted to let you know that the charges against me have been dropped. We can now put all of this behind us."

Could we? Would it be that easy? I grew up not knowing that my friend, my father's secretary's son, someone who I'd looked up to all my life, was really my half brother.

That same man had almost gotten himself, my father, and me killed. And for what? Revenge that he'd been fathered by a man who'd secretly taken care of him his whole life? Who gave him a trust fund worth millions of dollars?

I shook my head. It was always too easy for me to get caught up in what Brand had done and wonder what role I'd played in it. I'd finally accepted that I hadn't played any role. The choices he'd made were his own, and he would pay their price.

"Tara? You still there?"

"Sorry, Dad. I'm trying to finish a painting."

"I'll let you go. I love you, sweetheart."

"You too, Daddy."

29

Halo

Didn't matter what day it was; the routine was the same. I'd roll out of bed with the sunrise, have a cup of tea, and stare at the painting—the only thing that hung on the walls of my new apartment.

I'd moved back to Boston shortly after I returned from Italy, so it wasn't exactly new anymore. It just didn't feel like home. Had there ever been a place that felt that way to me? If there had, I couldn't remember it.

The night I'd landed in Boston, my sister picked me up at the airport. She drove to an out-of-the-way restaurant and, through many tears, told me she was pregnant. What she wouldn't tell me was who the baby's father was, or what her plan was for having him in her and the child's lives.

I was frustrated, but ultimately, all Sloane wanted from me was my support, which I agreed to give her. I moved from DC to Boston, held her hand when she told our parents, and went to her doctor's appointments with her. So often I saw her pain, the haunted look in her eyes that reminded me of Tara when I'd first met her. I wished she'd confide in me the secrets she felt she had to keep, but until she was ready, I'd be the best brother I could to her.

Yesterday, I'd received an email from Doc Butler, saying he'd be in town today and asking if we could meet. I'd anticipated hearing from him. In fact, I was surprised it had taken him this long to rescind the partnership offer made to me at the end of last year. I knew it was merely a formality, but once it happened, it would mean any ties I might have to Tara, even vicariously, would be gone.

I wondered if Doc was also meeting with Tackle, but not enough to ask. I'd see him later on the job site of the project we were working on together for his dad's company.

I took one more look at Tara's painting after I'd taken a shower, gotten dressed in the same crappy clothes I wore every day, pulled on my work boots, and left for work.

"Did you hear from Doc?" I asked Tackle when he parked next to my truck and climbed out.

"About?"

"He's in town. Wants to meet."

He shook his head. "Nope."

"Did you ever give them a final answer one way or the other?"

"Not yet."

I dropped the subject and went to work on the cabinet installation that was slated for today. A little after noon, my cell rang.

"Hey, Doc. You in town?"

"Just landed and got your email. Al Dente in the North End sounds fine."

I walked a few feet away from where my friend was working. "I know this is none of my business, but what about Tackle?"

"First things first. I'll see you tonight, Halo."

I walked up to the restaurant at a little before eight and saw Doc already seated at a table. He stood when he saw me walk in.

"How are you, Knox?" he asked, thumping my back when we hugged.

"Feelin' my age. Construction work is a lot harder than I remember it being. How are you? Merrigan? The baby?"

He laughed. "The baby isn't so much anymore, but thanks for asking." He pointed to a bottle of wine. "Can I interest you in a glass, or would you prefer something else?"

"Wine's good." That it was a Brunello di Montalcino made the ever-present ache in my chest hurt a little bit worse.

"How are you, Knox?"

"Been better. Been worse too."

Doc studied me. "Come back to the work you do best, Halo."

"Pretty sure that's what I'm doing."

"It isn't and you know it."

"Look, I appreciate this very much, but I screwed up seven ways to Sunday with Tara Emsworth."

"I'd say you've got a pretty good record, then."

"What do you mean?"

"Mine is way worse. I'd say my clean ops versus the ones I've screwed up are about fifty-fifty."

"That wasn't what I meant."

Doc smiled. "I know you didn't. But, Halo, we want you with us."

"Maybe this is none of my business, but I gotta ask. Why not Tackle?"

"First things first."

"Second time you've said that. What do you mean?"

Doc went to rub the back of his neck, but stopped short. "Tackle has some things in his life that he needs to deal with. He knows the offer we made him remains on the table."

Tackle had things in his life he had to deal with? Things I knew nothing about? I hated to admit it, but maybe our friendship would never be what it once was.

The waiter approached the table with a platter. I glanced in his direction and then did a double take.

"I took the liberty of ordering *antipasti,*" said Doc.

"White bean and prosciutto bruschetta," the man said, setting it between us.

When I looked up at Doc, he shrugged. "It sounded good. We can order something else if you don't like it."

"It isn't that," I mumbled, taking a piece after Doc had.

"Before we get back to the subject you don't want to talk about and I do, I want to give you an update."

I took a bite, marveling at how much it tasted exactly like what Nonna Bella had made for us the first night I met Tara. "On?"

"Brand Ripa was sentenced last week, and the charges against Richard Emsworth were dropped."

"Glad to hear it."

The waiter came back by and filled our wineglasses. "Are you ready to order?"

"Give us another minute," said Doc, not looking at the man. As soon as the waiter walked away, he leaned forward. "Get your ass back to work. And by work, I mean with K19."

I leaned forward like he had. "I gotta admit I don't understand why you're pushing so hard, but okay, I give. Under one condition."

"And that is?"

"My sister has some…stuff going on that I'm… helping her with. That has to come first."

He nodded like he knew what I was talking about. Shit, this was Doc. Maybe he did know. "Done," he said.

"Then, I'll sign."

Doc smiled. "Yeah?"

"Yes, sir."

He reached over to the chair beside him. "Let's finalize this." He handed me a copy of the offer they'd presented to me before. "Red line anything you want to negotiate."

"Is this the same as it was before?"

"For now."

I took the black pen from Doc's hand, flipped to the back page, and signed my name. When I handed it back to him, he smiled and reached over to shake my hand.

"Know what you want?" he asked, signaling the waiter.

I didn't bother opening the menu. "It's always better if you just let them bring whatever."

His eyebrows shot up. "Really?"

"Oh, yeah."

We were between the second and third courses when Doc leaned back in his chair. "There's something else we need to talk about, Halo."

I refilled my wineglass from the second bottle the waiter brought to the table. "How is she?" I asked.

"On the surface, Tara is doing really well. She's still living in New York with Penelope. And she opened her own gallery."

"Seriously?"

Doc nodded. "She named it the Catarina Benedetto Collection, or something like that. Anyway, I understand from Quinn that she's been doing a lot of painting."

"I'm really happy to hear that." Both that she was painting, and the name she'd chosen. It meant that her memories of the time she spent in Italy weren't all bad. "Where is it?"

"In Manhattan. One of those places where you need an engraved invitation to even get in the door."

Good to know, not that I would've considered just showing up.

Doc rested his arms on the table and leaned forward. "It's only because I love my daughter that I'm doing this. Got it?"

"Understood."

Doc reached over to the chair beside him like he had when he pulled out my K19 offer, and handed me an envelope.

"What's this?"

"Your engraved invitation."

"To what?"

"Tara's first show."

I opened the unsealed envelope and pulled out the card inside. "It's tomorrow night."

Doc nodded. "We'll all be there. Expect you to be too."

I put the card back inside. "Does Tara know I received an invite?"

When Doc shook his head, I tried to hand the envelope back to him.

"Then, I can't. I'm sorry."

"I don't ask a whole hell of a lot outside work, but I am now. As a personal favor, please reconsider."

I set the card on the table. "What if my being there ruins it for her?"

"Can you trust me?"

With my life, but we weren't talking about me. This was about Tara. I pulled the invitation back out of the envelope and read it over a second time. "You think a lot of people will be there?"

"I'm sure of it."

Maybe, then, she'd be so busy she wouldn't even notice I was there. "I'll do my best."

When we said good night, I walked the crowded streets of Boston's North End. Even this late at night, it was vibrant and bustling. I'd taken a car service, knowing how hard it would be to park in this area, and would take one back to my apartment in Back Bay later, when I walked off the angst I felt, wishing I knew what to do about Tara.

Countless times I thought about getting in touch with her, talking myself out of it an equal number. Whenever I was alone, I'd get lost in my head, replaying every moment I'd spent with her, wishing I had done it better.

I missed everything about Tara. I dreamed of her so often—her smile, her laugh, her soft skin, the heat of her body. Mine yearned to be near hers.

When I left Italy, she'd said goodbye, cutting me off, telling me not to embarrass myself before I could say…what? I couldn't even remember. That I was sorry. That I'd do anything if she'd forgive me for not protecting her, not believing her, not trusting she was exactly who my heart kept telling me she was, even though my brain fought so hard against it.

If I could go back and do it again, I wouldn't let her silence me. I'd tell her all those things. I'd also tell her the most important thing of all. That no matter how crazy it sounded, I loved her.

It wouldn't matter how much time passed or how long it was before I saw her again. We might meet one day, maybe as strangers, yet I'd still love her the same.

30

Tara

"Don't be mad," said Pen, who was practically tip-toeing into my studio.

"What did you do?"

She handed me an envelope. "Open it."

I pulled out the enclosed card and read the first line.

Please join us in celebrating the first US showing of artist Catarina Benedetto's Tuscan Collection.

"Are you *fucking* kidding me? Pen? This is in three days!"

"Is that all you're mad about?"

"You're kidding, right?" I sat down on the stool by the window and read the invitation for the second time, at least until the tears that filled my eyes made it impossible to continue. "Pen, how could you do this?"

"It wasn't just her." Quinn walked in the studio door.

"It was all of us." Ava and Aine followed her.

I hugged the invitation to my chest as tears ran down my cheeks. The simple truth was, if they hadn't done this, I'd probably be in my eighties and have ten thousand paintings lined up and still not have agreed to do a show. I looked into Pen's eyes first. "Thank you."

She raced over and hugged me. "You know we're doing this because we love you and are so proud of you."

"You really think I'm ready?"

"You're absolutely ready," said Quinn, hugging me like Pen had, except around her massive pregnancy belly.

"When are you due again?"

She rubbed her stomach. "This little nugget can make a showing anytime she wants *after* Friday. But to answer your question, not for another three or four weeks."

"And I'm a month after her," said Merrigan, Kade's wife, coming in through the open door.

"I can't believe my sister and my daughter are going to be the same age," said Quinn, hugging her stepmother.

"We might as well tell," said Ava, looking at Aine.

My eyes opened wide. "What?"

"Both of us are due in November," answered Aine.

"Except I've only got one in here," said Ava, pointing at her stomach.

"You're having twins?" squealed Quinn, rushing over to hug Aine.

"It looks that way," she answered, pulling out a sonogram photo and passing it around.

Penelope picked up one of my brushes and banged the end against the easel. "Ladies, need I remind you that Tara's show is in three days? We have a lot of work to do."

"Good thing we brought manual labor," said Ava, pointing to the door. "The guys are out there, waiting to do your bidding."

"Yes!" shouted Pen, pumping her first into the air. "Who've we got?"

"Tabon, Griffin, and Mercer for now. Kade is on his way," said Ava.

Pen grabbed my arm. "Come on, let's get this show hung."

"I just need a minute."

She nodded. "We'll start moving everything into the gallery."

Once everyone else was gone, Quinn walked over and put her arm around my shoulders. "Are you okay?"

"I'll be fine. A little overwhelmed is all."

"I understand. Just know that everything we're doing is because we love you *that* much."

I walked over, closed the studio door, and locked it. "There's something I need to ask you."

"Of course."

"I should've a long time ago, and I know this isn't the right time either, but I have to know."

She walked over and took both of my hands in hers. "Tara, what is it?"

"The missing money and Aine's bracelet—do you still think I stole from all of you?"

Quinn gasped and put her hand over her mouth. "You never got our messages!" She pulled me into a hug. "Oh, Tara, I'm so sorry, and I wish you had said something sooner. It was all a terrible misunderstanding. In fact, right after Pen left that message, Aine found the bracelet."

"And the money?"

Quinn nodded. "It's a long story, and it doesn't matter now, but yes, it was found and, again, a terrible, horrible, awful misunderstanding. Can you ever forgive us?"

"It isn't about forgiving you, Quinn."

We both jumped when someone pounded on the door. "Hey, open up! Feed us more paintings."

Quinn and I looked at each other. *"Tabon,"* we said at the same time.

"Your mother sent these," said Pen, bringing a giant bouquet of orange roses into the gallery office we shared. "Aw, that was sweet," she said, reading a card from the florist while handing me the other card. "Did you know that orange roses mean the sender is proud of you?"

"I had no idea." I opened the envelope and pulled out the card that said simply, *"I love you, Mom."*

"By the way, she did RSVP her regrets. She's in Turks and Caicos, and with the short notice and all…"

"She wouldn't have come anyway, you know, since my dad will be here."

"But the flowers are gorgeous, *darling*!" Pen said in her best impersonation of my mother. She handed me a glass of champagne. "Ready?"

"No."

"It's going to be amazing."

"Who is coming again?"

"Family, friends, the *Times* art critic, you know, no one terribly important. And don't worry, for tonight, everyone knows to call you Catarina."

Because of the scandal with Brand and my father, I'd made the decision to paint and open the gallery under a pseudonym. Deep inside, it wasn't the only reason, not that I'd let my mind drift in that direction tonight. I rolled my eyes. Who was I kidding? Every painting that hung on the walls of the gallery would send my mind drifting in that direction.

"Pen?"

She came back over and took my hands in hers. "You're ready. This is going to be amazing." She pulled a roll of stickers out of her pocket. "Red sold dots at the ready."

"I don't even care if anything sells."

Pen tucked my arm in hers. "I do! Come on, let's go downstairs and greet your patrons."

When we walked out onto the landing, the noisy room went silent for a couple of seconds before erupting into applause.

As I looked down at the sea of people, it was as though they magically parted, giving me a clear view of the man whose likeness hung on the wall in front of him. He turned then, and our eyes met.

31

Halo

There she was, more breathtaking than I remembered. Her deep blue eyes were piercing, as if she was waiting for my reaction, and then she looked away.

I looked back at the painting, the one of a man in a kitchen, the broad span of his back obscuring what was on the countertop where his hands rested. Besides me, only one other person knew what—who—was behind him.

When I turned back toward the stairs where she'd stood, Tara was no longer there. I desperately wanted to see the rest of the collection, the scenes she'd chosen to paint from our time together in Italy. It had been so brief, yet the memories were that of a lifetime.

As I'd feared, my being here did not add a happy memory. When I turned toward the front door to leave, I felt a hand on my shoulder.

I slowly turned back, capturing her wrist before she could withdraw her arm. I brought her hand to my lips and kissed it. I motioned to the red dot on the untitled painting's nameplate. "Please tell whoever bought it that I'll pay ten times what they did. A hundred times."

"It isn't for sale," she murmured.

I hadn't dropped her hand, and she didn't pull away, so I gave it a squeeze. "I haven't seen it all yet, but what I have is beautiful."

Tara's cheeks pinkened, and she looked back at the painting. "If it weren't for you, this dream never would've come true. Thank you."

"I think it would have, but for whatever small part I played, you're welcome. Seeing your work is such a pleasure, obviously not just for me." I motioned to the packed gallery.

"I don't care what anyone else thinks," she whispered. Her eyes were wide as though she hadn't meant to say the words out loud.

I leaned forward and brushed her cheek with my lips. "I miss you so much." I put my arm around her shoulders and turned us both toward the painting.

"I wish we could go back."

"So do I." I leaned my cheek against her hair, breathing in its scent.

"Catarina, there's someone—"

I dropped my arm, and we both turned. My eyes met Penelope's shocked ones.

"You're here."

"I am."

"I'm so sorry to intrude, but Mr. Farago would like a word." Tara nodded, and Pen looked back at me. "*New York Times* art critic," she whispered.

"Go ahead, I have lots to look at."

I was still studying the same painting when I felt another hand on my shoulder. "You made it," said Doc.

"Glad I did. Thanks to you."

"I have to admit, this one is my least favorite."

"To each his own."

"Why do I have a feeling it's the opposite for you?"

I shrugged. "Like I said…"

"Merrigan is waving me over. No doubt to buy another painting."

"How many have you so far?"

"As many as she wants."

Doc walked away, and I slowly made my way around the gallery. The next painting I came to was of the front of the farmhouse. This one, I had to have. I saw Ava, Razor's wife, and motioned to her.

"Hey, Knox. Glad you could make it. Tabon is around here somewhere."

"Thanks. I appreciated the invitation. Um, what do I do if I want to buy a painting?"

She reached into her pocket, put a red sticker on the nameplate, wrote a number on a small piece of paper, and handed it to me. "If there are any others, just flag me or Aine down. When you're finished, you can arrange payment with Quinn. You can't see her from here; well, maybe you can since you're so much taller. Anyway, she's in the back. Oh, and none of the paintings can be picked up until next week."

"Are a lot selling?"

"Oh, yes. Excuse me." She dashed off in the direction of another raised hand.

"I had a feeling you'd like that one," said Tara, coming up behind me.

"I like so many of them. Unfortunately for me, the majority are sold."

She leaned forward. "It's kind of crazy. I mean, I hope that people aren't buying them just to be nice."

I saw Penelope headed our way. "Listen, I know you've got a lot going on tonight, but I wondered if we could get together sometime."

"I'd like that."

"Should I call you?"

"You should stay a while."

I could do that.

32

Tara

"I'm sorry to keep interrupting you," said Pen, pulling me in the direction of a woman I recognized. Rebecca Elgin wrote for an international art journal and was widely known as an expert on Italian art.

"Ms. Elgin, may I present Catarina Benedetto," said Pen before leaving us on our own.

The next two hours were a whirlwind of people wanting to meet and talk with me. I tried to stay focused but found myself perusing the gallery to make sure Knox was still here.

There'd been so many times I wanted to ask about him, even contact him, but talked myself out of it. I'd pushed him away. How could I tell him I felt ready for him now? How could I even begin to explain?

Now, he was here and had asked if we could get together. I couldn't stand the idea of him leaving, saying he'd call, and then never hearing from him. That's why I told him he should stay.

With no one waiting to talk to me and the crowd thinning out, I made a beeline in his direction.

"I hope you're not getting bored."

He waved his arm. "I can't get enough. Each one is more beautiful than the rest. There are a couple I'm more partial to, however. I was hoping maybe I could get you to change your mind about selling that one." He pointed over to the one he was standing near when I first saw him.

"Maybe we could work out joint custody."

He laughed and looked around. "I didn't see your father here tonight."

"He was, briefly. It's my night and all."

Knox nodded, looking as though he'd run out of things to say.

"Come with me." I grabbed his hand and led him to the back of the gallery. I opened the door to my studio, not bothering to turn on the lights. I closed the door behind us, put my arms around Knox's neck, reached up, and kissed him. Our tongues wound around each other's, and I groaned. Knox put his arms around my waist, cinched up the hem of my short dress, and cupped the bare cheeks of my bottom. He spun me around so my back was against the wall.

"If I had known all you had on under this was a thong, I would've pressed you up against one of your paintings and done this." He kissed me again, his hands kneading my ass.

I reached up and pulled the strap of my dress off my shoulder, then pulled at one of his arms, bringing it to my bare breast.

"That is so fucking sexy," he murmured, latching on to my nipple with his mouth. "I love your tits."

When I heard footfalls in the hallway, I reached over to make sure I'd locked the door behind me. Knox pulled the other strap of my dress down and sucked the opposite nipple into his mouth.

"Every night, I dream of having my hands on your naked body."

"I dream that you're inside me."

Knox groaned and brought his lips back to mine.

"Make it come true."

He pulled back and looked into my eyes, illuminated by the light of the moon and the street lamps. "Now, Tara?"

"Now, Knox. Please, I'm begging you."

"I don't have a condom."

"I'm on birth control," I said, lowering my legs and pulling at his belt buckle. Knox put his hands on mine, stopping me.

"It can't just be this, Tara. I can't bury myself inside your warmth, walk out that door, and never see you again."

I grabbed his hand and put it between my legs. "You said once that I was yours and you were mine."

He slid one finger inside me. "I meant it."

"Then, hang on to me. Don't let me go."

Knox thrust a second finger into my pussy and, with his other hand, unfastened his belt and pants, letting them fall to the floor. I cried out when he withdrew his fingers and lifted my legs.

"Put me inside you."

I grabbed his hard cock and positioned it at my opening, moving my thong to the side. Knox thrust deep inside me and stilled. He rested his forehead against mine.

"Shh," he whispered. "Don't move, just feel how perfect our bodies fit together. I don't ever want you to forget this moment, Tara." He shifted so one hand was under my bottom. He cupped my cheek with the other.

I closed my eyes, focusing only on how Knox pulsed inside me.

"Look at me." His hand moved to my neck. "I love you, Tara. I don't want to spend another day without you in my life."

"Then, don't." I remembered Pia's words. "Run to love, to me instead of away, Knox."

His fingers pressed into the sides of my neck. "Say it."

"I love you, Knox."

Epilogue

Halo

"New York City, huh?" said Tackle, helping load boxes into my SUV. "Where are you gonna park this thing?"

"As if finding a place to park a car is any cheaper in Boston."

After he loaded in the last box, I set the wrapped painting, Tara's gift to me, on top. "Well, I better get on the road."

"I'm happy for you, Knox." We hugged and patted each other's backs.

"I have a favor to ask."

"What's that?"

"Sloane…she's going through some stuff." I kicked a rock near my boot. "It isn't my place to say what, but if you could watch out for her, I'd appreciate it. I'll be back as often as I can…"

Tackle looked like he'd swallowed the rock I'd just kicked.

"Look, if it's too much trouble…"

"It isn't too much trouble," he muttered.

"Thanks. So, I'll see you next week?"

"Wouldn't miss it for the world." He rolled his eyes. "I thought engagement parties were something only women did."

"It's a combination engagement, loft-warming party. And there will be beer." Something occurred to me. "You could always bring a date. Make a weekend of it in the Big Apple."

Tackle crossed his arms in front of him. "Yeah, maybe."

I climbed inside my vehicle, started the engine, and waved out the window as I drove away. As I turned the corner onto the main drag, I saw Sloane's car heading in the opposite direction. I honked and waved, but she didn't see me.

"Call Sloane," I said to the onboard computer.

"Hey, Knox," she answered.

"I just passed you. Did you need something?"

"What do you mean?"

"Are you headed to my place?"

"Oh! Uh, no. Just meeting a friend for lunch."

That seemed odd since it was ten in the morning. "I'll see you next week?"

"Wouldn't miss it."

I waited until I passed the exit for Worcester before I called Tara. "Hey, baby. I'm on my way. I got an early start. I'm about three hours out."

"Okay."

I smiled. "Whatcha doin'?"

She laughed. "Painting. Sorry. When did you say you'd be here?"

"Three hours. Should I go straight to the loft or stop by the gallery?"

"You can go to the loft. I'll, uh, meet you there."

"Sounds good. I love you, Tara."

"I love you too, Knox."

Two hours and fifty-seven minutes later, I pulled up in front of the Catarina Benedetto Gallery and parked in the loading zone. I punched the code into the keypad at the front door and walked inside.

"Hey, Pen." She looked up, waved, and went back to what she was doing.

I eased open the door of the studio, then closed and locked it behind me. Tara's back was to me, but I could see she had the end of the paintbrush in her mouth while she studied the painting in front of her.

I walked over to her, careful to make as little noise as possible, and wrapped my arm around her waist. She rested her hand on mine. "What did you do, fly here? What time is it?"

"One on the dot. Well, a little after. What are you painting?" It looked like something out of Italy, maybe even at Valentini, but nowhere I recognized.

"I don't know. I keep dreaming about you and me being in this place. I woke up this morning and knew I had to paint it."

"It kind of looks like a church."

"I was thinking the same thing." Tara dipped her brush in the water and then into the purple paint and added small flowers to a vine growing near the door of the building.

"But you don't know where it is?"

"No idea."

"Why do you think you keep dreaming about it?"

"You'll call me crazy."

I kissed the side of her neck. "Tell me anyway."

"I think it's where we're supposed to get married."

I pulled my cell phone out of my pocket and looked up a website. I clicked on the gallery page and scrolled through the photos. I held the phone in front of Tara, who looked at it, then at the painting and back again.

She turned in my arms. "*How did you find it? Where is it?*"

I swiped at the screen until it went back to the main page and then showed it to her.

"Oh my God, that's Valentini! How did you know?"

"I had a hunch. Is that where you want to get married?"

"What would you think?"

"It's perfect." I didn't care where the ceremony was. I only cared that Tara would be my wife.

"We should call Pia."

I pulled her closer to me. "Later."

"Yeah? What are we going to do now?"

"You're going to finish that painting."

"I am?"

I nodded and unfastened the buttons of her blouse.

"Let me guess. I'm going to do it naked?"

"You read my mind."

Keep reading for a sneak peek
at the next book in the
K19 Security Solutions
Team Two series,
Tackle's Honor

Prologue

Tackle

Six in the morning, and I was out wandering the streets of Boston's Little Italy, looking for a woman who didn't want me to find her. I walked past the closed-up shops and restaurants that dotted the first floor of buildings now labeled "live-work spaces" although I doubted a single business owner in this area lived in the luxury apartments above them.

There were worse neighborhoods where Sloane could've chosen to hide out. If, in fact, she was here. It was certainly understandable why it would've appealed to her. Mass General Hospital was within a mile's walking distance, and her office was even closer. Not that she was going into work very much these days.

She'd done a damn good job of disappearing in the couple of days I was gone, called away to take care of something I wanted no part of.

I hadn't seen or heard from her since the day I left the house I had been painstakingly renovating for us to live in. If she'd have me, which now remained to be seen.

When I said goodbye that morning, I had no inkling that when I returned, I'd find out she'd ghosted me.

"Sloane, where the hell are you?" I muttered out loud, scanning the high-rises as if she'd come out on the balcony of one and I'd spot her.

"You're too early if you're looking for Sloane," said a kid sweeping the sidewalk in front of a coffeehouse.

"You know somebody by that name?"

"Really pretty, stomach out to here?" The kid, who couldn't be more than ten or eleven, held his hand out in front of him.

Rather than respond, I took the photo I'd brought with me out of my pocket. "This her?" I asked, handing it to him.

"Yep. That's Sloane."

"Have you seen her?"

"I did the last two days."

"Where?"

"Here," the kid said, laughing as he swept dirt onto the street. "Comes down for breakfast, but not until later."

"What time?"

He shrugged. "Not before nine or ten, after the morning rush is over."

"You said she comes downstairs. Does she live in this building?"

"Anthony!" a man yelled.

"I gotta go. See ya, mister."

"Hey, wait!" I was too late. The kid was inside with the door closed behind him.

About the Author

USA Today and Amazon Top 15 Bestselling Author Heather Slade writes shamelessly sexy, edge-of-your seat romantic suspense.

She gave herself the gift of writing a book for her own birthday one year. Forty-plus books later (and counting), she's having the time of her life.

The women Slade writes are self-confident, strong, with wills of their own, and hearts as big as the Colorado sky. The men are sublimely sexy, seductive alphas who rise to the challenge of capturing the sweet soul of a woman whose heart they'll hold in the palm of their hand forever. Add in a couple of neck-snapping twists and turns, a page-turning mystery, and a swoon-worthy HEA, and you'll be holding one of her books in your hands.

She loves to hear from my readers. You can contact her at heather@heatherslade.com

To keep up with her latest news and releases, please visit her website at www.heatherslade.com to sign up for her newsletter.

MORE FROM AUTHOR HEATHER SLADE